THE FOUR HORSEMEN: CHAOS

L J SWALLOW

*V*EE

"*J*oss?" My voice sounds distant as if I'm somebody else trapped in a dream.

He doesn't respond.

I grasp Joss's hand and place my head on his chest, desperate to hear a heartbeat. Instead of the solid muscle I've rested my face on in the past, with his arms around me in comfort, I feel Joss's ribs against my cheek.

No sound.

My heart thuds in my ears as I pull away and look into his gaunt features.

Can I resurrect him with Heath's powers? Do I possess that energy? The adrenaline rushing through when I wanted to attack the creature has switched to panic, but however hard I concentrate, nothing is conjured in my mind and body apart from sheer terror.

I look between my hands and Joss, willing something to happen, but there's no spark or light. Nothing.

My breath shortens and I focus on staying calm. I can't panic; I need strength here. But how, when the person lying on the bed is an unrecognisable version of the man who held and loved me?

Has he died?

No.

This is temporary. Ewan's death was.

But how long until it becomes permanent?

Uselessly, I copy what Heath did to Ewan and place my palms on Joss's chest. I close my eyes and picture the afternoon in the car park basement, summoning to mind the light I saw in Heath's hands. My powers have triggered before, in self-defence, surely they will when needed to help one of the guys.

Bile rises in my throat when nothing happens. I push against Joss's chest, again and again, fooling myself if I press hard enough a miracle might happen.

Joss doesn't move. His chest remains still, and he doesn't breathe. Joss's heart doesn't beat beneath my palms.

Why? I have a close connection with Heath, and with Joss, but now I need the power from that connection and I'm failing. My determination to stay strong falls away and I gasp in a sob as my eyes blur with tears.

I'm wasting time.

My phone is downstairs so I search Joss's room for his. It rests on top of discarded clothes. A lump sticks in my throat as I remember him picking clothes from the floor the first night I stayed here. Joss, the guy who welcomed me and calmed me when my life disintegrated into the chaos now surrounding us all. The man who held me when I needed his gentle comfort.

Joss can't leave. He's part of me.

My throat tightens further when I see the picture on his lock screen. Us, the day we drank coffee and walked in the quiet countryside. I'm dressed against the cold, cheeks red, with Joss's arm wrapped around my shoulder. Relaxed. Happy.

Fingers trembling, I call Heath, almost misdialling, and he answers on speaker, the hum from a car engine drowning out his voice. "What's up, Joss?"

"Heath. Where are you?" I manage to keep my tone even, but my voice wavers at the end of the sentence.

"Vee? Are you okay? What's happening?" His question comes staccato, and I hear Xander's voice, fainter, asking the same.

"Something happened. Joss, he..."

"Joss, what? Vee?"

I stare at Joss's prone figure. "I don't know... A demon, I think... He died, Heath." The words spill, adding a finality to the scene in front of me. "He died."

The pause lasts a lifetime, and I'm terrified what they'll say to me.

Xander's voice interrupts us, his tone sharp. "Where are you?"

"In the house. What do I do?" My voice is small again, as useless as I am right now.

"What the hell happened?" Xander asks.

"I don't know! Please, tell me what I can do."

"Heath?" asks Xander.

"I don't know. Shit." My stomach knots as he pauses. "Have you touched him? Can you focus your energy on conjuring a light?"

"I tried, and I can't feel anything!" My anxiety peaks when he doesn't respond with anything apart from swearing. Is that it? Does this mean Joss has gone? "How long can he die for?" I rub my face at the crazy question. "Where are you?"

"On the way home. We'll be fifteen minutes," says Heath.

"Ten." Xander pauses. "What the fuck happened? How did a demon get in?"

"I don't know." I can't stop my garbled words as I stare down at a prone Joss. "Joss was upstairs, and I was downstairs with Ewan and—"

"You were distracted?" Xander's voice hardens. "Where's Ewan now? Tell him to put his clothes back on and help."

Wow. *Just wow.* I bite back an angry retort. "Ewan left the house. He wanted space."

"For fuck's sake!" For a moment I think Xander hung up, but the engine hums again as the dropped out reception returns.

Heath speaks. "Sit with him, Vee. Place your hands over his heart and picture it beating again."

I stare at my free hand. "I tried already! I tried to conjure your light, but it won't come."

"Try again," Heath says. "If you can't bring him back, he'll be fine. I'm not far."

"He won't stay dead?" I whisper.

"No. It might take him longer to recover, that's all."

A sob escapes, relief matching the anguish.

Heath's gentle voice crackles over the phone. "Vee, it's okay. We've got this."

"It's not bloody okay," growls Xander. "How did a fucking demon get into the house?"

J'm unaware whether the guys take ten minutes or fifteen because now I know how eternity feels. I do as Heath said, staring at my hands and concentrating with frustrated tears pricking my eyes when nothing happens.

I can't sense the demonic creature around anymore, but what if the apparition is hidden somewhere in the house?

I can barely look at Joss because he doesn't look like the man I saw an hour ago; he's a shadow of the man I love. Joss resembles images I've seen on TV news reports of starved people battling for life in third world countries. His ashen face is skeletal, cheeks hollowed, and closed eyes sunken into their sockets. Instead, I look at the window, holding his cold hand and willing the guys to hurry. The grey day descends into a dark evening, and my tears fall.

I hear the sound of a car skidding across the gravel driveway. A car door slams while the engine continues to run, then thundering footsteps sound on the stairs.

Heath careens into the room and over to Joss. "Move, Vee."

I'd be offended, but the sheer panic on his face is like nothing I've seen before, on his or anybody's, and panic stabs my chest too. A second set of footsteps run up the stairs, and a third set walk slowly.

Heath sits on the edge of the bed and holds out his palms, eyes closed, and the vivid light I saw him conjure the day Ewan died sparks in his hands. He performs the same action, drawing the light upwards with his long fingers, as if pulling the energy from his hands, and shapes the magic into an iridescent ball.

"Shit, he looks bad." Xander strides over and stares down, arms crossed. "Is he injured, Vee?"

"There's no blood," I say hoarsely and look up. Xander's eyes are fixed on Joss, and his wild-eyed expression terrifies me more than anything else today.

Xander's scared.

"He's not injured, but he looks like the life has been sucked out of him," replies Heath. "What did you see, Vee?"

I describe the scene to Xander and Heath, as Heath continues to expand his ball of light.

"He looks starved." Seth speaks from where he stands in the doorway. He holds the doorframe on either side, as if holding himself out of the room.

Nobody replies as Heath finally slams both hands on Joss's chest. I cover my face, peeking through my fingers, willing Joss to move as Heath sits hunched over with his hair falling forward into his face. The light surrounds Heath's hands and spreads across Joss's chest; Heath's breathing becomes laboured and he swears, pushing his hands against Joss in the way I did earlier.

"Heath?" Xander steps forward. "Isn't it working?"

Heath doesn't respond and squeezes his eyes closed, shutting us out. I startle as a rush of life flows into Joss, jerking through his body, and his eyes snap open as he draws in a loud breath. Heath removes his hands and his shoulders slacken, but Joss doesn't move. As he stares at the ceiling in silence, the dread rises again. I can't sense his emotions. Where's his relief? Confusion? Pain?

Anything?

Xander wipes a hand down the side of his face. "Joss."

No movement.

I voice the words I sense in the air around me. "Didn't it work?"

Heath takes Joss's pulse. "It worked. Joss is alive, but maybe he's stuck."

"Stuck where?" I look between him and Xander.

"In the dark." Xander's response is curt, and he leans over to examine Joss. "He's alive and breathing. Let him rest." I'm relieved Xander has snapped back to the War I recognise as he takes control of the situation. "Vee, sit with him, and we'll check if whatever attacked him is still around. Heath, come with me."

I turn my attention back to Joss. *The dark?*

"And phone bloody Ewan. Tell him to get his arse back here."

"He won't answer if he's riding," replies Heath.

Xander swears under his breath and shoves past Seth to leave the room. I watch him go. Like Seth, I haven't moved from the one spot since Heath and Xander arrived in the room. I still can't move because if I do I might fall.

I stare at the carpet, and when Heath's arms circle me, I allow myself to let go of the tension as he hugs me to him. "You look worried. He'll be fine."

I grip him in return, burying my face into his chest and focusing on his cologne, a reminder of happier times. "What does Xander mean by the dark?"

"I don't know." His voice is muffled by my hair. "I haven't died yet."

Yet. I tighten my arms, ear pressed against his heartbeat. I feel his worry. Today I showed Heath I couldn't save him if he dies, the way I assured him I could.

Ewan needs to listen to me. I need to be whole.

2

J OSS

he shadows clear, and the world from my visions sharpens into focus.

The dark street smells rank; a nearby skip overflows with boxes and refuse adds to the piss stench. I'm jittery, tensed and scouting out the area as I walk towards the high-rise block of flats.

Two kids sit in the dirty stairwell, smoking and drinking. Not even teens. Eleven years old maybe? They nod at me in recognition, but edge away as I pass them.

The fucking lift is broken again.

As I stomp past the kids and upstairs, I stare down at my dirty jeans and tattered black and white Converse. Thank fuck I have the energy to climb ten flights of stairs tonight.

My phone sounds and I pull it out, sliding nicotine-stained fingers across the screen. Aimee. Another in a long line of increasingly urgent messages asking me to call her.

I scroll through the recent ones; I'll reply to those worth my while later. Four flights into my ten-flight climb, I pause and place a hand on the stairwell. The rush in my bloodstream still misses something, and I pull a packet of smokes from inside my leather jacket.

One lit, and between my lips, I keep going.

I reach Aimee's floor, step down the familiar hallway, which shares the same delightful sight and scent of poverty. Some doors look like they were kicked in recently, probably by the residents too.

I'm glad I worked my way out of this fucking hellhole.

I keep my finger on the doorbell, which buzzes incessantly. Half the time the fuckers are too out of it to hear me. Their loss because I'm not coming back again. They waste my fucking time; they can find another dealer.

I pull my finger away and rub at the indent the button left on the tip.

Fuck this.

I drop my cigarette butt to the floor and lean against the wall to check where I'm due next. Seriously, the arsehole who's supposed to do my run tonight had better watch his back, especially if he's stolen anything.

One more try.

I press the bell again, this time stopping and starting like an alarm.

Someone shuffles along the hallway. Normally she shouts but today, silence.

The door opens and Aimee regards me. I remember when she was hot, could pick and choose from the clients lining up. Now most of them come from me, desperate to feed her addiction, taking anything she can. Her gaunt face and over-dyed hair join her half-starved, addicted body.

"You're a fucking mess," I tell her. "Put some makeup on, for fuck's sake."

She's not scared of me, not anymore. She doesn't feel anything, I'm sure. She gave me her money, her youth, her life; Aimee is a shell of the girl I knew from school. I stare at her puffy face.

"You've been crying? What happened?"

"Chanelle." She wraps her thin arms around herself, wide-eyed like a trapped animal.

Instinctively, I step in front of the doorway and shove it closed behind me. "What? Did she leave? I warned her what would happen if she did!"

Aimee shakes her head and a tear flies across her cheek. "She's..."

"She's what?"

Aimee points toward an open doorway.

I walk into the lounge room, trashed, a stolen TV in one corner and a stained mattress in another. The place is usually full of stoners, who'd be homeless otherwise. Not today. A girl is slumped on the sofa, on her back and a slack arm hanging over the edge.

Fuck.

I've seen this enough times to know what I'm looking at.

"How long?" I growl and stride over.

"I don't know," replies Aimee in a meek voice. "Is she dead? She looks dead."

I chew a nail. Fuck. "Maybe. OD'd? Does she have a pulse?"

Looking at the state of her, I'd lay bets there's no maybe here.

"You know she's dead." I spin around at the voice from

behind and a guy stands in the hallway. Tall, hard face with a nose broken too many times. Tattoos cover his skin, on his neck stretching towards his cheek.

Gun pointing at my face.

"You killed my sister last week with your poisonous shit, you evil bastard. She was getting herself clean and you fucked her over."

I reach into my jacket and close my fingers around my gun, but this guy isn't here to negotiate, or waste his chance.

Gunfire sounds and the shadows swallow my life.

3

*V*EE

I lie with Joss on his bed, gripping his fingers and listening to his slow and steady heartbeat, terrified it might stop. His hand warms in mine as the minutes pass, and my heart slows as exhaustion replaces the adrenaline. I curl myself around Joss, wishing I could burrow into his soul and pull him out of wherever he is. He's alive, but he's lost somewhere. Is he in the place he told me about, the one from his visions?

The bedroom curtains are open and the night now blankets the countryside surrounding the house and intrudes through the window. Shadows are cast across the room from the tree outside, and I shudder at the memory of the wraithlike figure.

I doze. At one point I hear Ewan's motorbike but don't wake fully until I'm aware of Joss's arms around me. Warm, strong. Shifting from his arms, I touch Joss's face. He's my

Joss now—cheeks no longer sunken and colour in his face. I kiss the lips no longer blue and hold my mouth there for a few seconds, desperate to give him my affection and love.

I move away and stroke his face. "Are you okay?"

"Kind of. Feeling like Death."

I push myself up on one elbow in panic. "You feel like you're going to die again?"

His mouth tips into the Joss smile I've missed recently, and the shadows of my day finally break. "Nah, like Death: lost in my thoughts and a bit emo." I poke him. "And what do you mean 'die again'?"

"You weren't just sleeping, Joss."

"Oh? But I was dreaming." He bites his lip. "I think. Did anybody see the demon this time? Was I imagining it?"

Joss's brow tugs deep as I describe what I saw. "The guys think it was a wraith or something. Where did it come from? Did you see it attack you?"

"I saw shadows. Sometimes wraiths attach themselves to people, but I should've sensed if that's what happened. Did you kill it?"

I scrunch up my face. "No. Sorry."

"All good." He kisses my nose. "They're hard to kill anyway. I expect the guys got him."

I can't tell him they never found the creature or know exactly what it was.

"I think it was with you for a couple of days, Joss."

"Maybe. I wasn't feeling good."

"That's an understatement. Are you okay now? You don't feel distant again?"

"No." I feel like he wants to say more but stops himself. This isn't the time for questions, but for solace and to share the emotions I have for him. The ones I swore I wanted to lose.

Whoever or whatever did this to Joss did us all a favour, because however horrific the last few hours were, I know I could never stop loving and caring for this man—or any of them.

I snuggle my head into the crook of Joss's neck and place my lips on his skin. "You scared me, Joss. I'm glad you're okay."

"I'm bloody hungry. Tell Xander he has to cook me something." Joss's warm breath tickles my hair as he chuckles, stepping further to his old self and away from the one over the last few days.

"I'll make you something."

Joss reaches out to me when I stand to leave and holds out a hand. He grips my fingers and, although he smiles, the haunted look in Joss's eyes follows me from the room.

*E*wan, Heath, and Xander are all in the house, but not together.

Bad sign.

I pass Joss's study, and through the open door can see Ewan at the dark, wooden desk. Should I talk to him about what happened between us earlier? The events since put things into perspective for me, did they for him?

My stomach flutters as I watch him. In just a black T-shirt, his tattooed arms are visible and the sleeve stretches tightly across the bicep inked with vibrant patterns and pictures I've never seen long enough to figure out. One day, I want to explore them with my fingers as we cuddle. My heart twinges. Whatever else I want from him, his affection is one.

I love the way Ewan sometimes mouths what he's

reading onscreen, or the peace he seems to get from spending time away from us in his own world. I surge with the need from before, but also remember the hurt caused by his words.

As if sensing me, Ewan turns his head. I expect him to glance away again, but I'm the one who can't hold our mutual, confused look.

"How's Joss, Vee?" Heath walks from the kitchen. "I heard someone come downstairs and wasn't sure who."

I break my gaze at Ewan. "He's okay. Tired and hungry. How are you?"

"Okay. Tired. I think helping Joss took it out of me."

I play my fingers across his lined face. Exhaustion has crept up on him over the recent days, and resurrecting Joss has intensified the dark circles building beneath his eyes. "You should rest."

"Yeah." He holds up a beer and winks.

I give a wry smile. "I said I'd make Joss something to eat. Are you hungry too?"

Heath follows me as I walk into the kitchen and hovers next to me as I open the fridge. Beer. A loaf of bread. Milk. I guess chasing assassins and demonic forces doesn't leave much time for grocery shopping.

"I'll order pizza then?" says Heath from behind.

I search the cupboards too and manage to locate a half-eaten packet of chocolate biscuits. I push one into my mouth, just to make sure they're fresh, of course.

"Where are Xander and Seth?" I ask through mouthfuls.

Heath leans against the counter next to me. "Xander went for a walk, and Seth's in the lounge, avoiding us as usual."

"If he's brought some gear from his place to our place,

Seth's accepting he'll stay around," I suggest. "That's a good thing."

Heath drinks and then wrinkles his nose. "I suppose."

"You don't trust him either."

"Come on, Vee. How do you expect us to? He's bloody weird, and I don't understand how he found a lot of his info. And what about the passports his friends had but not him? Something's off."

I admit I wondered about this, but with everything happening, I haven't asked him. I will. "He's helping, that's the main thing, Heath."

"Hmm." Heath strokes my hair. "Forget him. Tell me how you're feeling. That must've freaked you out before."

"What bothered me the most was I couldn't do anything. Why couldn't I? I thought I had your powers now."

"Yeah." Heath drains his bottle and sets it on the table. "I think that one takes time to develop. It takes a lot more from me than zapping people. Perhaps you're not magically strong enough yet?"

"You know the truth here, Heath. You said it yourself. This comes down to me 'assimilating' as you put it." I pause. "I suppose Ewan told you what happened between us before."

"Kind of." I roll my eyes at his evasive comment. "I don't know the answer, Vee. None of us do."

I suck on my teeth. Seth isn't the only one the guys don't fully trust here, and that hurts. Yes, I don't know what will happen if I have sex with Ewan, but I can't imagine I could stop caring for the guys. The bond wouldn't break; it would strengthen.

Wouldn't it?

But I can't deny the drive inside to be the one to take control of them all and call the shots. The thoughts in the back of my mind push through sometimes, and I struggle to control an itch I can't scratch. This has grown worse since sex with Joss, and the growing control I've gained over Xander.

But they wouldn't love me if I was a threat; they'd surely be aware of that.

I hold up the biscuit packet. "I'll take these to Joss. You can order us all pizza."

As I walk upstairs, the bizarre switch between the ordinary and the supernatural follows me. And the fear I'll fail if I don't harness every power the guys have.

4

*V*EE

*U*nable to stop worrying about Joss, I stay with him into the night and hold him as tightly as he holds me. I left him sleeping once the sun rose, and while I ate breakfast, Xander quizzed me. I run through every detail again and again for Xander and the others, but they can't figure out what attacked him and how.

The determined, confident Xander who resurfaced yesterday has retreated again; I've never seen him this quiet and introspective. I waited to talk to him last night when I ate pizza with Heath and Ewan, but he didn't return from his walk for over an hour. I gave up waiting, left some pizza for him, and took the rest up to Joss.

Xander calls a meeting, as expected, as soon as Joss feels ready. He's brighter already, in his colour and in his mood. Still, I sit with him, holding his hand, acutely aware how the prospect of losing him sharpened everything into a new focus. They need me to be Vee, and I need them.

Joss faces the same questions he can't answer, and the quiet frustration grows. One step forward, another back. Just when we had a lead.

"We need to focus on following the new leads," says Joss eventually. "I think what happened to me was to distract us. Let's not allow that to happen."

Seth stands in the corner, away from the table as he watches and listens.

"Your codenames seem to be significant." He breaks his silence and reddens when everybody turns to look at him. He chews a nail. "You call yourselves the Four Horsemen, right?"

"Correct," replies Ewan.

"And you said something attacked you, Ewan, and they were diseased. Like zombies."

Joss sighs. "They weren't zombies. Zombies don't exist."

"Really? But demons and fairies do? Am I supposed to be selective about what I believe in?" Seth shakes his head.

"Fae. Not fairies. Read about them," replies Xander.

"Sure, give me my laptop back, and time to myself, and I will." His mouth thins.

Ewan shrugs. "Sure. You can have it for an hour."

Following their altercation the other day, Ewan changed his mind and took Seth's laptop back. Is Ewan's control over Seth belligerence or fear at what he'll do?

"So yeah, you call yourself Pestilence." He continues his hard stare at Ewan. "You were killed by something diseased, if I'm to believe you died."

Ewan's brow furrows.

"And you call yourself Famine, right?" He nods at Joss. "When I saw you yesterday afternoon you looked starved."

"Shit." Joss rubs his face and looks to the others. "It wasn't just an attack yesterday. I didn't feel right after what happened at the storage unit, as if the last few days I was slowly starved of emotions, until I stopped feeling altogether."

I clasp my hands together under the table. "Joss is right. He faded."

"Fuck. I hate to say this, but Seth could be right," mutters Xander.

"You think someone is targeting us with our own powers?" asks Ewan. "How? We're stronger than that."

"Yes. And we've been told that Seth's assassin was killed by a primordial magic that the oldest entity we know doesn't understand. We're dealing with something different here."

My mouth dries at Heath's words. We've found a few connections over the last day, but the idea someone is using the guys' powers against them isn't pleasant—or beyond possibility.

"But we didn't die," says Ewan. "We're okay."

"This time." Heath's voice is quiet. He stares down at the table. "If I'm next, what then? Whoever this is could pick us off one by one, and if they start with me..."

They all die.

Again, nobody has a comeback or answer and I swallow hard. "But Death can't die, surely?"

Joss blows air into his cheeks, and Xander's face holds a deep concern, one too familiar since yesterday. Ewan stares at a spot on the wall, away from everybody.

"We don't know that," says Heath eventually. "Maybe I've been lucky. I've been close in situations, but the guys managed to intervene before it was too late."

I will one of the guys to come up with an answer, to

encourage Heath he'll be okay, but nobody responds until Seth speaks again.

"I thought Vee had all your powers. Why can't she fix you, or whatever, if you're hurt?"

"I don't have his resurrection power." My words sound weird spoken to Seth. "I mean... I can't help them."

"Why?" he presses. "Can you learn or something?"

"Maybe," says Joss.

"I didn't learn the others. I have some of their powers, but not the same strength, or all of them."

My neck prickles, and I side glance Ewan who continues to stare into space. Is he the answer to my gaining full strength?

Seth approaches to sit at the table, at a corner and away from the others. "How does this all work? You never told me exactly *what* you are. You told me about demons and vampires, and I've seen evidence of enough to know there are strange things in the world, but who are *you*?"

I look to the guys, almost for permission, and Heath nods. "You've heard people call me Truth?"

"Yeah, but that's because of your name, isn't it?" asks Seth.

"I'm sort of the fifth Horseman."

Seth snorts a laugh. "Okay...."

"Are you going to listen to her or not," growls Xander.

"If you can believe the guys have abilities that aren't human, then you can believe that I have some of each of them. That's part of the reason for our relationship and why I'm with them."

"You mean your weird polyamory thing?"

"Not relevant," snaps Ewan.

Oh, but it is.

Seth takes off his glasses and polishes them on his shirt,

lips pursed, before he places them back on, as if this makes the situation clearer.

"So are you genetically modified or something? Like military experiments?" He pauses and smirks. "Bitten by a radioactive spider?"

"What the fuck are you talking about?" asks Ewan.

"Doesn't matter." He sighs. "Well, I guess you have to figure out what's trying to kill you."

"You think?" says Ewan, voice laden with sarcasm.

"And—if I understand this correctly—you have to find some magic... thing. Do you think this Alasdair guy has something? Like, in his house? Shouldn't you look?"

"We hadn't thought that far ahead. We've been a bit distracted by demons invading the house and killing us!" retorts Xander.

"And that assassin woman. Can't she find it for you?"

Xander rests back in his chair. "I see you've been thinking about all this."

There's less nervousness around this Seth, no staring at the floor or his hands. He smiles at the guys, and I sense triumph that they're listening to him.

"I have a lot of time to think. I'm quite analytical, you know. I absorb a lot of information and have a photographic memory." He gestures at Xander's phone. "Like with the rune. I memorise everything I think will be important, and secret symbols top my list."

"I thought that was unusually impressive." Ewan crosses his arms. "Coincidental even."

"You all say I'm weird. I am. I know that. People have told me that my whole life, but at least my screwed up brain is useful." Seth mimics Ewan in crossing his arms.

"So, Seth, since you're knowledgeable about the

situation, what would you do next if you were me?" asks Xander.

Seth bites back a smile. "I wouldn't want to be you, Xander."

"Hypothetically." Xander's face darkens and I tense. Is Seth pushing his luck here?

"I'd ask Syv for help finding this magic item. I'd try and arrange a meeting with Alasdair and find more about his link to these other gangs you keep mentioning." He points at me. "And I'd do everything you can to give Vee all your powers."

"That was my plan." Xander taps his fingers on the table. "I already called Syv."

"Oh?" I look to him.

"The next logical move."

"And you think she'll help? She didn't seem very co-operative," I reply.

"She'll help." Xander's voice is firm. "I'll tell her the stakes."

"Did you arrange to meet up with her?" Heath asks.

"Yep. This evening. La Fee Verte."

"Let me guess," puts in Seth. "That's where the fairies like to hang out."

Ewan's sour face lights up with amusement. "I would absolutely love to see you walk into that place and call one of them a fairy, and manage to walk out again uninjured. They hate it."

"But isn't she a demon?" asks Seth, ignoring Ewan. "You said the fae gang don't like the demon gang."

Joss tips his head. "They're not 'gangs', they're races. And for someone who's hardly said anything, you seem to suddenly have a lot of opinions, Seth."

"You're the ones who said it was in my interests to stay

with and help you. That's what I'm trying to do! If this means I can live my life again when everything is sorted, I will."

"So you're sticking around?" asks Heath.

"Yes. By choice this time. But this trust needs to be mutual. Ewan, could you return my laptop and phone please?"

Ewan straightens in his seat and looks to the others. "Guys?"

"Can I say something?" I interrupt. "We need to lay this animosity between you and Seth to rest and cooperate more."

"Thank you, Vee." Seth's voice is low and he smiles in gratitude. "I appreciate that."

The following silence isn't very encouraging.

"Are we all agreed we visit Syv tonight?" asks Heath.

"I suppose I need to go too?" Seth asks Xander. "Under your watchful eye."

Once over, Xander would've retorted, but the defeat surrounding him concerns me. He was upbeat about the possibilities ahead, but now his confusion is all I can pick up. I can't let him slide too. I need to speak to him.

5

*E*WAN

I once thought Vee consumed my thoughts and interfered with my ability to think straight, but that's nothing compared to what's happening now. She's in every dream, enters my head whenever I'm unfocused. Hell, she unfocused me. Each time I'm close, I want to talk to her, apologise, tell her how I feel. But that's the problem. I can't reconcile how I feel to what she wants. Am I being selfish? Is my refusal to give in to the need to unite, to cross the line and feel her beneath my body, my hands, losing herself with me inside her causing more than sexual frustration like none I've ever experienced?

I've fought my craving for Vee, and it's grown into an intense hunger gnawing at the shackles I've put on myself.

Vee's hurt because I'm avoiding her, but what else can I do? Until I've figured this out in my head, until I believe that I won't fuck everything up, I have to. One touch, one moment alone together, and there's no way I'll keep this under control.

But something else holds me back. I need Vee to want me as Ewan, not just to fulfill what she believes is some weird destiny. I don't know how she responds to the others; it's not something we talk about, beyond the fact her powers intensified. Does Vee look them in the eyes with affection, does she tell them how she feels, or is this only physical pleasure for her?

Hell, Vee's so much more than that to me, and I want her to know I love her, and for her to love me back. This screws with my head even further. Girls never affect me like this. Sure, most have been random hook-ups with no desire to go further, but not one girl ever triggered a need to be around them, to have their attention, the way Vee does.

I want to believe this is more. I need to believe this is human Vee wanting me. Am I fooling myself?

One thing: since our conversation, when I rode away sick to the stomach for hurting her, Joss says she hasn't spoken to him about losing her emotions again. Does she realise she doesn't want to? Or is it because she can't?

Is it because I can't finish the job and make us whole?

Mindfuck.

I sit in the kitchen, elbows on the table, head bowed with my fingers in my hair doing a bloody good impression of Heath. Xander and Heath went to meet up with Syv. Xander said to 'ask for her opinion' on what Portia's asked, but I know what that means. I don't want to be dragged into something else. Whatever happens, our names had better be kept clear too.

The fridge door opens and closes, but I don't look around, until I sense whoever is in the room doesn't move. I let go of my hair and twist my head.

Seth grips a bottle of water and watches me warily. He jerks backwards as I move. Does he think I'll smack him? Good. He needs to be kept on his toes, and worry what I'll do to him if he steps out of line. I don't care what Vee says, I trust him about as much as I do fae. He has some qualities in common with them: the evasiveness, the clever questions, the ability to turn conversations in the direction he wants. If the others paid more attention, they'd see this too.

What if the reason Seth was targeted has nothing to do with us? That he's hiding with us for another reason?

"Are you okay, Ewan? Did something happen? I don't know where Xander and Heath went."

Yeah, because we didn't tell you.

"I'm fine." I keep my voice gruff, with a warning look that he shouldn't pursue his questions.

"Can we call a truce?"

I blink at his words. "I thought we already had."

"I'd call it an uneasy stalemate."

"Call it what you want. I'm not on your back anymore, am I?"

"No, but you watch me. You don't trust me."

"Yep. Sorry." I push my chair back and stand.

"Why?"

"Reasons."

"Wow, Ewan. You're not very eloquent, are you?"

I stand over him. I'm not much taller, but my solid build eclipses his wiry frame. I've itched to get in Seth's face and ask him questions, but never found him alone. He'll be sorry he walked in and interfered in my day.

"I don't know who you are, or what your game is, but when I find out, you're fucked."

Seth's mouth parts and his cheeks redden. "My game is

to help you. To find proof someone is killing people - and to find out why."

"Sure."

"What have I done, Ewan? I don't understand. I gave you all the information I have. No wonder Vee struggles!"

I straighten. "What the hell is that supposed to mean?"

"I've noticed how you avoid her. Vee gave up a lot to come here and help you all, and I can tell she's struggling with your behaviour." He pauses. "You guys keep saying she's the centre of your world, but all I see is her being pushed to the edge."

I swallow down the harsh response springing to my lips. Seth's doing the same thing again. He's interfering and subtly planting thoughts, all with a feigned innocence. "You don't know anything about our lives," I reply in an even tone.

"Really? Because I'm currently forced to live your lives, and it's shit."

I'm tempted to tell him to piss off and try his luck alone, to see how long he survives, but my suspicion steam rolls those words. Seth wants me to say that.

"I don't think you're who you say, Seth Marks."

Seth removes his glasses and polishes them, as he often does when wanting to pause a conversation.

"That's your call, Ewan... what was your name again? The false one you have?" He places his glasses back on. "If anybody isn't who they say they are, it's you and your band of brothers."

I fight down giving him the angry reaction he wants and maintain a game face to match his.

"You've dug deep into my records and my past, Ewan. It's all there. Seth Marks exists. Do you? Who are you, code name Pestilence?"

I bristle at his mocking tone. Cheeky fucking... *My bloody fist could show him I existed.* "Me? I'm one of the people keeping your sorry ass alive right now."

"So you keep saying."

"But I'm watching you, Seth. You don't fool me."

Slowly, Seth unscrews the bottle and swigs, his eyes on mine the whole time. *Yeah, I'm onto you.* He wipes his mouth and screws the lid back on. "I think it's quite sad how little you trust people. Even the girl who loves you."

"I hope you're not bullying Seth again, Ewan." Vee walks into the kitchen. "Have you seen my coat?"

I point at her green jacket slung over the nearest chair and back away when she approaches, avoiding her eyes.

"All good. You know how Ewan is, Vee. It's hard to connect with him sometimes."

Vee laughs and swings the jacket around to push her arms through the sleeves. "He's the strong silent type, for sure."

"Where are you going?" asks Seth.

"For a walk. I want to catch up with Xander while he's in a good mood."

Seth nods. "Good plan."

I say nothing as Vee takes one last glance at me before heading out the door. Seth watches her go, too intently for my liking.

He flicks his fingers after Vee. "That was a perfect example of what I'm talking about. Is it jealousy? Don't you like Vee having sex with the other guys?" I narrow my eyes, and his mouth twitches into a smile. "Are you scared she'll compare you all, and that you won't measure up to the others?"

"You're a devious fucker," I growl. "And you're bloody

lucky I'm in a good mood or I would've spread your nose across your face by now."

"Raw nerve?" He chuckles. "I don't care what you think about me. I'm just doing the same as you all do. I'm looking out for myself." With a tight smile, he grips his drink and walks out of the room.

This guy must have a desire to feel my fist in his face because I won't let him get away with this sneaky-ass behaviour much longer. I don't care who the fuck Seth says he is, when I get the opportunity, he's out of here.

6

XANDER

I hate that the guys know I'm struggling if I take longer walks than usual, but we all are so I can't be singled out. Normally I save long walks for crisp, sunny days, but today I risk the threat of rain to walk off as much nervous energy as I can. I shove my hands deeper into my pockets and burrow my face into the top of my jacket. Fuck, it gets colder. Next winter, I'm making sure we're overseas.

Joss sat me down earlier and talked me through the confusion, calmed the desire to charge from the house and react, instead of planning. I'm pissed off that there was no sign of whatever attacked Joss, and even more that something breeched our defences. Why didn't Joss know he contained something demonic?

That leads to a worse thought: was it demonic? Although we spent hours searching and not finding the thing, I'm bloody relieved Joss is back to normal, the way Ewan was.

But Seth's words resonate. He's correct.

Who's next? How can we stop it?

What if Heath dies?

I arranged our meeting with Syv for early evening, when the club will be emptier. She hangs out in there a lot, as do some of her clients. They allow her, because she has too much information on some of them. Then, we pay Alasdair a visit. He doesn't work at Nova Pharm, and he lives in Scotland. There's no address for Myriad Foundation's offices, but I'm sure Ewan can locate him.

I should be lifted by the news, but all I can picture is Joss last night and fight something I haven't experienced before —doubt.

Add to this that the Collector knew Horsemen before and doubt grows into a deep uncertainty in the pit of my stomach. I always knew we weren't the first, but is this how they died?

Will they kill Vee too?

Vee, the girl walking across the freezing ground towards me. My heart rate increases the closer she gets, and again I'm reminded her power over me isn't just as Truth, but as a girl who's begun to possess me: heart, body, and soul. She's dressed in skinny jeans and heavy boots with a padded green jacket, a usual look for her, but today there's a black beanie pushed onto her head.

Her green eyes stand out against the black, and the way her hair is pushed around her red-cheeked face gives her an innocence that reminds me further that she's human.

I'm not in the mood to talk to anybody right now; my head doesn't know which direction to turn in.

I moisten my cool lips as she stops in front of me, my

desire to reach out, touch her face, and kiss her growing with the warmth in my chest. Instead, I grip the lining in my jacket pockets.

"What happened?" I ask sharply. "Is everybody okay?"

She nods. "I came to see how you were."

I frown. "Me? I'm okay. Pissed off all this is happening, but also happier things are progressing."

Vee taps her lips and hesitates before saying, "I wanted to spend time with you when you're calm."

"I'm never calm." We exchange wry smiles. "Especially not around you."

"The only time we talk, we argue. I want to change that."

I look down in surprise when Vee links her arm through mine and tense, unsure whether to move her arm and push her away, or allow myself closer.

"I guess. Like with Seth, it's important we build some trust."

She laughs up at me. "Are you comparing us to you and Seth?"

"No. You know what I mean." I pause and she remains close, closer still as she looks up at me.

I love and hate how Vee makes me feel, how my whole body fills with heat when she focuses her attention on me; how my thoughts scatter and are replaced by nothing but the desire to be naked with her.

To love her.

I look away in case Vee reads this in my eyes.

I fight so fucking hard not to touch her skin, to allow myself to be pulled into her, but I fail.

I cup her face. Okay, but I won't kiss her. "What's really wrong? Why did you come out here?"

"Do you think it's possible for me to develop Heath's power, and keep you all alive?"

I blink at her forthright question. "I don't know. I hope so."

The conversation falters until Vee says, "You haven't asked me how I am recently, Xander."

I swallow. "How are you, Vee?"

"Confused. I had an argument with Ewan about the situation."

"Ah, the wanting to stop feeling anything? The guys told me about that." I've had the conversation with Joss. With Ewan. With all of them. I pretended it didn't bother me and told them I wasn't surprised because I've seen a harsher side to Vee. But I am because I've also seen tenderness in how she treats us all.

"But that's the problem now. I don't want to lose the positive emotions, so I can't lose myself, can I? Does that mean I can never be as powerful as you? Never have Heath's power to save you all?"

I drop my hand. "Save us all? You're not here to do that."

"How do you know?"

"Don't be intense right now, Vee. I can't cope with anymore of this, my head's fucked."

I temper my tone but her eyes reflect hurt. "This is important, Xander."

Has she backed down on the idea she should be emotionless? I had the feeling Ewan's reaction affected her. Good. But there's an uncomfortable side to this situation: her need to physically bond with us. I'm convinced *that's* where her power lies.

I can't tell Ewan to have sex with Vee; that's unreasonable and totally weird, but I think it would help. I don't share their belief she'll destroy us. How can she? As long as those emotional responses to us remain, so will Vee.

"I don't understand what you've come here to say to me."

"Will you stop shutting me out?"

"I don't shut you out."

Vee shakes her head and takes my hand from her face. She squeezes my fingers. "It's good to talk to you when you're not shouting at me."

I don't know how to respond to her following me and trying to dig into my thoughts and feelings. What does she want here?

"Yeah, well, you haven't pissed me off recently."

"I think I should be the one pissed off. You hid from me what happened to Joss at the storage units. You said no secrets."

I pull my hand from hers and keep walking. "You know why."

"Because you don't trust me, either?" She remains a few steps behind, not following, and I stop too, then turn around.

My heart wrenches at the look on her face. Hurt. Why can't she be angry, and then I can end this conversation with strong words and an excuse to walk away? Instead, Vee fights tears.

Crap.

I stride back over and look down, hands in pockets. Her eyes glisten and the friendly smile from a few minutes ago has been replaced by a downturned mouth.

"I find it hard to trust anybody apart from the guys. I still don't understand who you are and that messes with my head." I run a palm across my hair. "I'm sorry."

A tear escapes Vee's eye, and instead of wiping it away, she lets it trail down her cheek. This is worse than any argument I've had with her. Vee has never cried in front of me. I clench my hands in my pockets, unable to decide whether to run from the empathy clouding my head, or step away from my safe place and closer to her.

"Sorry," I repeat to save saying anything else.

She remains looking at me steadily. "At least you're all honest about *that*. I love you all, and this is how you're treating me."

Her words knock me backwards. She means as friends, right? As the group she lives with?

"I don't believe you're dangerous or want to hurt us, I just don't trust people. End of."

This time she swipes the tear falling. "We're part of each other, Xander."

"I know."

"So does that mean you don't trust yourself?"

What the hell is with all this heavy shit? Heath will listen to this; I need to move on.

"I suppose it does." Will this appease her? Stop this?

"Liar," she says with a small laugh.

I can't figure out what she wants here. Is Vee expecting me to break down and tell her how I feel? That I'm prepared to allow her to overcome more of me?

I freeze as she steps closer and places ice cold fingers on my jaw. "I wish I could see inside your head sometimes. I pick up on how you feel, but you're hard to read."

Her touch and the affection in her eyes intensify the swirling confusion and my racing heart. "Let's just be happy we're not fighting."

She moistens her lips. "Our fights always end in interesting situations."

An image flashes into my mind. Several images, ones that follow me into my dreams at night with the reminder how the intensity between us with sex is like nothing I've experienced before. And how I wish I could drop some of that for tenderness.

"True."

She laughs. "You're a man of little words—sometimes."

"Then don't try to push them out of me."

She strokes my scruff with her thumb, watching the movement, and I suddenly realise I'm lost in one of the moments I imagined.

Vee and Xander, not War meets War.

"I want to know the man beneath the facade. I want to be with him."

So do I.

"Maybe when this shit is over and things calm down, we can have this conversation."

"Things will never calm down, will they?"

Each word she speaks, every unhidden emotion she shows, pulls me further apart. I'm not used to moments like this, and I want to fight instead. When I clash with Vee, we don't think. We don't talk. We just do.

My mouth dries as the moment intensifies. *Don't kiss her. Don't let go.*

I close my eyes and when I open them again she's closer, her mouth millimetres from mine. The spark between us is almost tangible, and the hesitation something new. Normally our mouths crash together in frustration and need, but now all I want is her mouth soft against mine, and not hard and demanding.

I take Vee's face in both hands, intending to move her lips away. The fact her skin is smoother than I remember, her eyes filled with more than raw desire, ends my resolve.

Our mouths meet in a gentle kiss. I take time to relish how she tastes, how soft her lips are as they gently move against mine. This kiss delves inside and Vee pulls a new part of me into her. Not my War, but the love hidden inside and denied.

My life changed when I met Vee, but more than I expected. I've had to admit to myself, Vee is more than a weapon to help us and more than the infuriating girl I battle to control. She always held a piece of mine, but I need to give her more.

There's no breathless lust or battle for the upper hand unleashed by our kiss. Something different takes hold, and the bonds holding my emotions unshackle as Vee's touch pulls them away. This time I want to hold and love her, not fight until we release our frustration.

This is what I never wanted, but always craved.

Vee pulls away first, pink cheeked, tears still held in her eyes. She touches my lips. "I wanted you to know I care about you, Xander. Thank you for showing me how you feel." Her smile joins the bright day in lifting the shadows. "Maybe one day you'll tell me too."

Over the years, I've learned to read people's eyes, searching for their intent. I know that as much can be spoken with a look and a touch as with any words, another reason I avoid both.

"You know I care about you," I say my eyes silently telling her more.

"And I care about you too."

She emphasises the words *care about*. We both know the truth runs deeper, but for now those words are as far as we go.

Without her lips on mine, I'm snapped back to our other reality. "We have shit to do."

"Of course." For one awkward moment I think Vee's about to hold my hand to walk back, but she loops an arm through mine again. "Let's get back to the shit we have to do."

With the freezing day heated by Vee, and the world suddenly twice as confusing as ten minutes ago, we head back to the house. Side by side. Silently.

7

HEATH

La Fee Verte.

I stand with the others and examine the facade in front of us. To humans, the darker side street between the main road and the shopping area behind appears nondescript. The building itself looks like an unused clothes shop with printed signs in the window stating "closing down sale" and the glass doors filthy. The place is sandwiched between a tattoo parlour and a pub, useful for disguising the strange mix of people who hang around outside.

A glamour prevents humans seeing the true venue, but it's one all supes can see past. In unglamoured reality, the building has the same front as many clubs throughout the local towns, including a sign lit in green neon with the name. They have guys on the door to warn off any non-fae who try to gain entry. Most wouldn't be stupid enough to try.

Dodgy shit happens here. Human clubs have their drugs and dealers; fae clubs have dealers too, but they trade in magic.

Generally, we ignore the subculture created by the fae who attend the club. They're no threat to anyone but themselves. This is where the vicious element of the fae hangs out, those who embrace the darker uses for their magic and shun the world. Light fae such as Portia claim superiority and self-control; but scratch the surface, and you'll find the same malevolence in them. Fae can manipulate and confuse, harm those who anger them, and many have no qualms about killing other kin who stand in their way of ambition and greed.

We last visited here to speak to the owner when we initially looked into the Portia plot, in case someone here was connected, but these fae are too stoned on magic to give a shit about anything.

Every fae visiting the joint knows who we are and will avoid us if necessary. We're not concerned with fae, or their activities, unless we detect something more sinister around. We're more bothered by activities at the Warehouse since humans and supes both visit the place and humans could be targets.

We've met Syv here before. Although we keep ourselves and activities strictly separate, she has extra knowledge about underground activities in the supernatural world. This helps when the forces connected aren't visible in the human world. In the past, we've contacted Syv for the lowdown when we have names that need tracing, but often we can't find her. She's not entirely reliable anyway.

Taron's death brought us back together, and I hope this means she'll help out rather than disappear.

The narrow venue contains four floors. Two hold small dance floors and bars, the other two a quiet "chill out" area, and at the top, the room used by Mac. He's another fae who goes by a single name, no doubt due to his profession.

I've met him, and he's basically a stoner and a dealer who holds enough sway over the club to have his own quarters. The clients he attracts pay a large entry fee, and indulge in alcohol, so the gig is mutually profitable.

We're not entirely sure how or what magic is dealt, nor do we care. The Horsemen aren't here to police this shit.

Portia's court pretend the addicts don't exist, and they barely do. Hell, the idea they could cobble together any kind of plot against others is laughable. These fae are too stoned on magic to give a shit about anything. They're so far on the fringes they're falling off the edge into oblivion caused by their addiction. Us? We have more important things to deal with than fae social issues.

Especially now they want fuck all to do with us.

Xander strides through the crowded entrance, jostling past fae taking up space in the small hallway as they stop and chat. Nobody looks at us as we pass; I avoid making eye contact with anybody, but as Seth trips after us he fails to hide his open-mouthed staring at the bizarre outfits and hairstyles.

I've never been in the presence of so much latex and leather in my life, and definitely not around as much naked flesh. A girl beside me wears so little it's a good thing the tattoos cover enough skin to give her some modesty.

I follow Xander into the brightly lit bar area filled with loud music and louder hair colours. Xander's arranged a meet with Syv in a quieter bar area on the third floor, and we push through to the narrow staircase. The small room we reach has walls painted in purple with murals of forest scenes. People are draped on sumptuous sofas, around tables holding drinks, some talk in soft voices, others stare into space, hypnotised by the lyrical voice in the music playing.

Syv lies horizontally across a sofa close to the bar, jacket under her head, holding her phone above her head and texting. Her hair hangs half way to the floor, and her motorcycle boots rest on the other sofa arm. She turns her head and watches impassively as we approach.

"Wow, you're all here, including your pet human. I didn't realise I was so alluring."

She saves her sweetest smile for Seth who grins back like an idiot at her seductive tones. He stumbles back to sit on a nearby sofa, and Vee sits beside him, Ewan on her left.

"We're sticking together right now," replies Xander and looks down at her. "Move so I can sit. Please."

"Buy me a drink." She smiles up at him. "Please."

Syv knows how to push Xander's buttons, but who doesn't? Try to control the control freak and watch the sparks fly.

"Joss." Xander doesn't turn around.

Joss mutters something about being his slave and stands. Seth shifts along the sofa, closer to the sofa Syv sits on, transfixed. I've no interest in her—never have—and find her choice of dress amusing. It takes something to be able to pull off the leather pants look and not appear tacky. She also wears a tank top with low cut arms, revealing her naked side and a black bra strap. Several necklaces hang around her neck, some spoils she's kept for herself from her travels. Are they magical? I'd lay bets at least one must be.

Syv's tempting to many, but hates male advances. Not

that she invites many, unless she's in the mood. I've never seen her with any guys apart from Taron and Abel, but I have no interest in her personal life.

I never had any interest in her, either.

Judging by Seth's goldfish-faced staring at her, he does. Now that would be something bloody funny to see—Seth flirting with a chick. I've watched for signs he's attracted to Vee, and if he is, he keeps his thoughts well hidden.

Syv sits and swings her long legs around, facing us, and Xander places himself sideways on the sofa to look at her.

She tucks her phone in the leather jacket pocket and looks around. "Your visit to the Collector went well, I hear."

"Did you look at the images I texted to you before?" Xander asks.

"Yep."

"And?"

"I've not seen anything like them before. Col told me they're older than him and not fae. They don't look demonic to me either."

I smile to myself. She has to be one of the only people who calls the Collector anything but his full name.

"But have you looked for magical items as old before?" I ask.

"Yeah. They're harder to find. Mostly amulets, fetishes, and shit that have a connection to my clients' races. For example, I know if I'm looking for a fae item to look for particular gems or talismans depending on the court. This? Sometimes hidden in the weirdest items. I've found old bones with this type of rune carved, but also located something inside books. There's no knowing what to look for." She pauses. "Humans like to put things in museums, which is bloody stupid on their account as anybody could take them."

"Anybody such as you?" asks Ewan.

She winks at him.

"How do you know where to look for things?" asks Vee.

"If I have a lead, I follow it. I have a skill for detecting magic sources around. Put me in the vicinity and I'll know." She pauses. "It's acquiring them that can be the dangerous part, and I'm skilled in that area too. Hence, I'm expensive."

Joss reappears from the bar with three drinks. He passes a small glass containing clear liquid to Syv, a glass to Vee, and sits with his beer.

"Where's ours?" asks Ewan.

"Oops I forgot." He grins before swigging from the bottle.

"We found the rune used in a human company logo. Have you heard of Myriad Foundation?'

"Nope." She drinks. "What is the Myriad Foundation?"

"We're still investigating exactly what they do, but it's community-based projects of some kind. Helping the homeless or something."

"How cute."

"We have some people's names and want you to see if you recognise any." I pull a folded sheet from my pocket and pass the paper to Syv.

She holds it between two fingers and scans the words. "Nope."

Xander huffs and rests back.

"I'm unclear exactly what you want me to do. Find someone or find something?"

"We need you to search for anything that could be linked to the runes. A cypher. A book. Anything at all."

She hands back the paper. "Yeah, that might be wasting my time. I'm on another job right now."

"Doing what?" asks Ewan.

"Collecting." She gives him a sweet smile. "I want out of this shitty winter. I'm leaving next week."

Shit.

"We can pay for you to stick around," says Xander. "This is important and not just to us."

"Yeah, but, Xander, everything's always important to you guys. What makes this so different?"

"Someone's trying to kill us," says Joss.

"And? That's not new either."

Xander flashes Joss a look. "Surely you realise if someone is using magic this old, then they could be more powerful than anybody we've come across before."

Syv wrinkles her nose. "Possibly. Or this could be someone who thinks they can wield the magic and ends up killing themselves. Problem solved."

"I admire your optimism," I reply.

Syv sips her drink, sizing up the situation. "I might be able to spare some time to help. If you can get me an 'in' to the place, I'll scout around before I leave." She pauses and flicks her fingers. "Then, if I think there could be something to investigate, I will. Cash upfront."

"Yeah, right," scoffs Xander.

She places her glass down. "Suit yourself. Maybe when I return from the States I can help you then."

I throw Xander a look as she stands.

"Wait. Okay. How much?"

"Ten thousand."

Ewan chokes on his drink and Xander's lips thin as she waits.

I glance at Xander. "Sit down. Let's negotiate."

Syv drains her glass and rubs her lips together. "Sounds good. Maybe we should all get some more drinks."

"I'll get them. Ewan?" I incline my head towards the

nearby bar. Most in the room are sitting, leaving the barman with elbows on the table and a glazed look. I'd say boredom, but I'm unsure who's drunk or if they're using the magic dealt here.

I haven't had a chance to speak to Ewan about recent events. I know Xander has, and he's concerned something still bothers him.

8

*H*EATH

I wait with Ewan at the bar, aware how much we stand out even without being the Horsemen. Some of these fae know who we are; others don't care. As we order, another guy as tall as us but with half Ewan's bulk approaches and ensures he's as far away as possible from us.

"How's things?" I ask Ewan.

He continues to stare ahead and a muscle ticks in his jaw. "I'm good. Eager to move on and find out what's happening. And fix it."

"I'm still freaked out over what happened to Joss. I've never had to use as much magical energy to bring one of you back before."

Starting Joss's heart again was bloody hard. This time, it was as if he needed my physical energy too to make the cold, clammy skin warm beneath my hands. A weakness spread back through my arms in return, and all I wanted to do afterwards was rest.

"I think he's okay now." Ewan nods at the white-haired bartender as he places the first of our drinks order on the bar. "I also think Seth's right. Someone is using our powers against us. That worries me."

Not as much as it worries me. I want to comment with my fear about myself and what happens if Vee can't use my resurrecting skills, but Ewan's touchy about the situation. There's an unspoken tension between the four of us that his decision to keep his hands off Vee could be slowing us down.

I glance back to the others, where Seth sits bolt upright, hands on his knees. He watches everybody who passes before turning his attention back to the spellbinding Syv. She can tell he's smitten by her; Syv's used to attention, and I'd love to see how he'd respond if she took the next step into teasing him.

"How do you feel about our hanger-on now?" I ask Ewan.

He takes his beer and turns to rest against the bar, facing our group. "Seth? I still don't trust him. Do you?"

Good question. Sometimes, yes. Others, no. I've worked amongst humans, whereas the guys haven't, and I've come across weird guys like him before. I always wondered what went on behind their eyes and below the surface, but they never hit my radar enough for me to bother. Seth is helping us, but there's an agenda beneath that help.

"Haven't you noticed his sly attempts to come between us?" continues Ewan.

"I think that's because he can see a weakness. I'd be pretty pissed off if I was being dragged around by people who don't trust me. I'd probably try to piss them off too."

Ewan makes a *humph* sound and swigs from his bottle.

"If he steps out of line, I'll be down on the guy like a ton of fucking bricks."

The man at the bar wanders off with beers in his hand, and he's replaced by two girls. These fae don't keep their distance, and they shuffle towards us. One bumps me, and I turn my head. Two slender girls with the pink hair and glitter-covered skin smile up at us; their faces and eyes are as identical as their clothes. Twins? One sidles closer and runs her fingers along my cheek, mouth curling into a seductive smile.

Classic fae behaviour. No personal boundaries.

I grab the girl's wrist and pull her hand away. "Bad luck, if you're here for an easy hook-up, move on."

She peers at us through the dim light, then grips the other girl's arm and her voice pitch rises in delight. "Lizzie, they're two of the Horsemen."

Oh crap. Seriously, once-over I enjoyed the rock star reaction to us, even though I'd never touch a fae.

"Oh, wow!" breathes out Lizzie. "Why are you here?"

Ewan straightens and looks down at her. "How old are you?"

"Twenty." She fights a smile. "Almost. I'm Stella."

"I've seen you around before," he replies.

I groan inwardly as Stella twirls hair around her finger. "We are memorable, I guess."

"Heath. They were in pictures with Elyssia at the Warehouse, back when we were looking for clues about the demon guy who attacked Portia." He points between them.

"Are you friends with Elyssia de Court?" I ask.

The glances they exchange already answered my next question. "Is she with you tonight?"

Stella shakes her head. "No."

"Maybe we should ask Vee to question them?" Ewan says. "She'll know if they're lying."

Lizzie interrupts. "We haven't seen her for a few days. She's been fighting with her mum, badly, and she's threatening to leave."

"What?" I straighten. "When did she say this?"

Lizzie shrugs. "Dunno."

"When did you last see Elyssia?"

The bartender places two bottles of brightly coloured alcohol in front of Stella, and she switches her seductive smile to him instead as she hands over cash.

"We're not her keepers." Lizzie, takes a bottle. "She prefers humans anyway. I've no idea why she's spending time with Mac and—ouch!"

Stella interrupts by stamping on Lizzie's foot. "We don't know where she is or what she's doing. I don't understand why Elyssia is so interesting to you." She pouts and straightens her already flimsy top, revealing more flesh than appropriate. "Is it because she's a princess? You know she's not the only beautiful fae, right?"

I sigh. Ah fae, and their modesty.

"Is Mac here?" snaps Ewan.

"Mmmm." Stella licks her lips, mouth parted with pleasurable memories. "Oh, yeah."

"They're addicts," I say to Ewan.

"We're not! We just dabble." Lizzie giggles, grating my nerves.

Fae elders are aware of their teen faes' activities, but they are powerless to do anything apart from educate their offspring. If fae authorities did crack down, the club would burrow deeper underground. We toyed with the idea that Elyssia may've met her demon buddies there, but demons could never gain entry to the place. The fae would know straightaway who they were, and they wouldn't survive. One thing they do share with their light kindred is a hatred of demons. Syv must have something over the owners if they let her half-demon self into the joint.

"So Mac's in tonight?" he asks and points to the top of the building.

The girls nod, and I sidestep them. "We need to speak to him."

Stella smiles up at me. "Does fae magic work on Horsemen? Did you want to try some out?"

"No. Excuse me." I attempt to move, but Stella remains still. She traces fingers across my chest, biting her lips as she moves them downwards. "Impressive."

I scowl at Stella and shove her hand away. I'd be angry, but there's also something amusing about her self-assurance.

Ewan doesn't share my thoughts. "Go away, little girls," he growls.

"Fine." Stella drops her interest as quickly as I dropped her hand. She tips her chin. "I bet you wouldn't be as miserable if you were less frustrated. If you change your mind, we can help with that *issue*."

"And I bet your parents wouldn't be happy you're here. I can find out your names." Ewan's sour face is enough for them to step back. Without another word, the pair hightail it from the room with their drinks.

"I think we need to check the place to see if Elyssia is around," I say.

"Not my monkey, not my problem," mutters Ewan. "If Portia needs help, she'll ask us."

"Will she?"

"C'mon, Heath, I don't think the fae queen needs help controlling anybody."

"That's not what I mean. I know Elyssia is an immature pain in the arse, but the fact she's young and stupid is what causes problems."

"Like I said, not my problem. Come on."

I swear the fae girl was about to out Elyssia for spending time with the drugged fae element. If she has a dealer, I bet he doesn't know who Elyssia is.

Either that or he doesn't value his life if he's screwing around with Portia's daughter.

"No. We need to check." I head towards the open doorway and into the small space between the stairs up and down.

"Wait, Heath," he calls. I stop on the steps, one hand on the wall and look back. "Let me tell Xander where we're going."

I crane my head to look for the others. They're still positioned around the table. Although many would think Xander's relaxing, he's on alert, taking in everything happening around him and who's coming and going. I admire his calmness tonight—how long will that last?

I give a curt nod and rest my back against the wall.

*H*EATH

*T*he stairs stop abruptly in a low-ceiling area, where a row of wooden chairs line the dark-blue painted walls. Two men sit on seats outside Mac's room, and the black door, which almost blends into the wall, is shut. I expected bodyguards or some kind of security, but the only people here are fae kids sitting in silence as if waiting at a doctor's surgery.

A guy with spiked, blue hair and enough metal in his face to make cutlery from stares at his shoes; the other rests his head against the wall and stares upwards. He looks human, but I don't think he is, just a fae who normally blends himself into their society.

"I don't want to waste my time on this." Ewan walks straight by and yanks at the door handle. The metal-faced guy jumps to his feet as he begins to open the door.

"I'm next! And you can't go in there without an

appointment." Desperation fills his voice, not anger, but if he confronted Ewan bets are off who'd win.

With a disparaging look, Ewan slams his palm on the door to open it and walks through. He immediately stops and I have to step to one side to avoid walking into him.

A man looks up in surprise, dropping his attention from where a girl straddles his lap, lying backwards against his outstretched arms. The pale blue magic swirling like a cloud around his fingers touches her chest, above her breasts, and a glow surrounds her face.

For one shit moment, I worry I walked in on him screwing someone, but she's wearing black skinny jeans. Instead, this looks like at bizarre lap dance.

How the hell does she sit on him at that angle and not fall backwards onto the carpet?

The man's sitting, but his height is apparent. He's dressed in a suit, a grey shirt unbuttoned at the front. Short dark hair is pushed upwards into a quiff, and his eyes glow the same colour as the magic. The blue light surrounding him strokes his high cheekbones and emphasises the otherworldly look beneath his human appearance. His chest rises and falls rapidly, but he's composed. In control.

The small room's walls are painted black, and the energy from the magic fills the space. I'm not susceptible, but the intensity hurts my head, a static pain behind my eyes.

Continuing to watch us, he strokes from beneath the girl's chin and along her neck, the blue cloud following the line of his fingers. A murmur escapes her lips and her eyes are closed in a weird ecstasy. This explains the girls' aroused state earlier.

"Can I help you?" he asks, nonplussed

I've met Mac a couple of times, and don't like the guy. He's a predator. The guy maintains his youth by exchanging magic with these people to gather his own strength. In return, he infuses them with ancient magic that many fae can't access. This stronger magic has been lost through generations, and few still hold it. Some would argue at least he's not using it for destruction, but here he is destroying fae lives.

The youngest fae generation don't care about their magic power, most preferring a human existence, and some trade for a taste of ancient magic. Powerful, mind-altering, and addictive. The newer fae then lose their magic power as they siphon the spell energy to the dealer, who uses it to keep himself strong.

"We need to talk to you," says Ewan.

"Will this wait? I have a customer."

The girl shifts against him and runs fingers through her long white hair that almost touches the floor, she leans back that far. I blink. The magic's holding her up. This isn't sex, but I'm bloody uncomfortable watching.

"The sooner we talk, the sooner we can leave you to your "—Ewan screws up his face as he looks at the girl too —"activities."

"Her time's up anyway." Sliding a hand behind the girl's back, he draws her to him, and the girl's head lolls on Mac's shoulder. "Give her a few minutes to come back to us."

The girl willingly gives herself, but the scenario creeps me out. If we ever mend ties with Portia again, I need to ask her why she allows this.

"For fuck's sake," mutters Ewan and turns away.

The girl's unaware of us as if she could float out of the room. I imagine she would since she's shimmering with the high he infused into her.

"Can I take a rest in your bedroom?" she whispers and runs a hand coyly along his jacket.

Mac takes her hand and kisses the back. "Not tonight, beautiful."

"Please." Her attempt to look coy is lost in the drugged expression.

"Not tonight." His voice lowers, firmer, and she climbs from his lap with an apology. *Don't upset your dealer.*

The girl finally notices us and turns a lazy smile our way. "Enjoy," she murmurs as she leaves.

Mac laughs softly and sits back on his seat. "Why are you here? You can't trade with me."

"We're not here for *that*," Ewan snaps.

The blue in his eyes fades back to a normal shade, and he taps his lips with a finger. "Is this about the humans trying my magic? I thought you didn't interfere. Nobody is getting hurt."

"What the fuck?" I ask. "You'd better be kidding me."

He flicks his fingers dismissively. "Most only try once because they can't handle what I give them. Besides, they have no magic to give in return."

I snort. "But they have money."

"Yes. I suppose they do." He rests back. "They enjoy other pleasures with the fae, so experimenting with magic isn't unusual."

"No race is to coerce humans through deception," growls Ewan.

Mac snorts. "They don't remember anything when they leave. Really, you're worrying about nothing."

"If we catch you harming humans, you know what the answer will be." Ewan crosses his arms. "A painful one for you."

"Okay, okay. Hint taken. I'll back off them, okay?" He cranes his head towards the door. "Can you leave? I'm busy with clients."

Firstly, I don't need Vee here to know the guy's lying about backing off on a lucrative market, and secondly his attitude towards us is about to cause problems.

"We're looking for Elyssia de Court," Ewan says. "Has she visited you?"

A door at the opposite end of the room clicks, and a girl stands in the doorway. Her hair has escaped from the long blonde plait, and she holds a T-shirt in her hand, sinking against the doorframe as she waves it at her dealer.

"Babe, is this mine?"

My eyes are involuntarily drawn to her, because show me one guy who can't when a seminaked girl walks into a room. Not that I've any interest, especially when a second later I meet her eyes.

Ewan beats me to it. Mac doesn't need to answer our question.

"Elyssia?" The girl's glazed look retreats and she steps back slamming the door. Ewan's there in seconds, pushing his way through.

"Okay," I snarl at the guy. "What the fuck is *she* doing here?"

"Who? Annabelle? She's a close friend." His mouth spreads into a smile. "Well, this week she is."

"Uh. Right. She's not Annabelle. *She's* Elyssia de Court."

He straightens and blinks. "What the fuck?"

"Yeah, y'know... the queen of this realm? Her daughter."

He springs to his feet, and I sneer at the cocky attitude evaporating. "I didn't know!"

"You don't know who Portia's daughter is? Give me a break."

"I don't know what her bloody offspring look like. I don't pay attention to what Portia does unless I need to. I ignore her, you know that."

I laugh. "Yeah, well I don't think she's gonna ignore you when she finds out about this."

Mac drags his hands down his face. "Fuck!" He follows Ewan and flings the door open. "Get her out of here! Now!"

A trembling Elyssia sits on the bed, T-shirt now on, arms wrapped around her legs as she looks up. "No. Don't make me leave."

"Elyssia. You need to," I say attempting to temper my tone.

"I'm not going home!" she says. "I won't go back there! She wants to send me away. I'm not having guys chosen for me, and I'm definitely not marrying one of them."

I exchange a glance with Ewan. Elyssia ran away? And Portia never told us?

"I don't want you here," growls Mac. "You fucking lied to me! Do you know what could happen now? Shit!"

"My mother doesn't care about this place; she'd never know I was here." Elyssia narrows her eyes at me. "If *you* hadn't come here, I could've moved on."

"It's a bloody good thing we did!" snaps Ewan. "Get off that bed, now."

"You don't tell me what to do!"

"Okay. I'll call your mother then, should I?" Ewan puts a hand in his back pocket.

She stumbles to her feet. "No! Okay. But don't take me back to her."

As if we have any choice.

Mac holds his hands up, palms out. "She's nothing to do with me anymore. Take her."

I grit my teeth at how dismissive he is, but I bet I don't have enough fingers to count how many girls he's had in this bed in the last week alone.

"Didn't you notice her magic was stronger?" snaps Ewan.

"Hey, some kids have stronger magic if they're bred right. I just thought she must be from a purer line."

I wish Vee were here to spot if he's lying.

$\mathcal{V}$ EE

$\mathcal{H}$eath appears and leans down to whisper something to Xander. Xander's face hardens, and Joss shifts closer to catch the conversation.

"Trouble?" asks Seth and takes a nervous glance over his shoulder.

"Maybe."

"What is this place? There're some seriously weird people here. I swear half of them are on drugs."

Nobody pays attention to Seth, whose interest in his surroundings grew after Syv left with assurances she'll help.

Xander walks away with Heath, and Joss shuffles over. "They just found a certain fae queen's daughter."

"Elyssia?" I burst out. "I bet her mum isn't happy she comes here."

"Nope. Especially as she was in bed with the fae's premiere magic dealer."

"Wow. What's happening?"

"They've gone to collect her. Hopefully Xander won't need to carry her out over his shoulder."

I chew my lip at the imagery. Yep. Could totally see that happening.

Xander reappears with Ewan and a girl. Ewan's hand grips the girl's arm who stumbles as she walks through the doorway towards us. Last time I saw Elyssia, she was pinned against her lounge room wall by a demon. This time, she's the image of teenage rebellion, dressed in tight, deliberately distressed clothes and her white blonde hair trailing from the ponytail around her heavily made-up face.

And either drunk or high.

The unimpressed girl pulls her arm away from Ewan's grasp as she approaches and rubs her eyes.

"We're taking her home," says Xander, tone short. "Come on."

"Oh no, you're not taking her," replies Heath. "You're the last person Portia wants to see."

"I have her daughter!"

"Exactly. I'll go with Ewan."

Elyssia sinks onto the sofa and rests her head back, staring at the ceiling. Xander sits opposite, elbows on knees. Is he waiting for her to try to run?

"Why's she here?" I ask Ewan. "Does Portia know?"

"Nope. She's run away from home."

"Oh." I look at her. "Why?"

"Remember Portia said she was sending Elyssia away? Yeah, well Elyssia doesn't agree with arranged marriage. Fae kids spend time too mixed up with humans these days, and then they don't want to play their roles. Especially fae princesses. "

Poor girl. How old is she? Nineteen? I know she finished school recently. I can't imagine any of her friends are facing exile.

And I don't want to think what Elyssia is facing when she's delivered home by the Pony Boys.

10

HEATH

I park my car outside Portia's house. Each home in the street is still and quiet, but I know Portia's will be on alert.

I look over my shoulder at Elyssia, who's slumped against Ewan's shoulder. "Wake her up."

Ewan scrunches his nose. "She's a little too friendly when I do."

I can't help laughing. "I'm sure you can defend yourself."

"Do you know how uncomfortable it is that both mother and daughter sexually harass me?"

"You're hilarious! Poor Ewan." He pulls a face as I laugh at him.

"She's barely twenty years old!"

"Ah well, at least she's not a teenager."

"Gross, Heath."

Ewan shifts away from the princess, and Elyssia's head

lolls sideways as he moves.

"Hey! Sleepy head! Time to go home."

Her eyes flutter open. "What?"

"We're home. Your mother freaked out when we called her. Prepare yourself."

"Oh shit." She rouses herself further and sits. "Please stay with me."

The girl's a bedraggled mess. More hair escaped her ponytail and her make-up smudged into dark lines on her cheeks. Her clothes are creased, and she faintly smells of the sickly incense from the club.

"How did you think you could get away with trying to leave?" I ask.

Elyssia unclips her seatbelt. "How would you feel if you were forced into a life you never asked for?"

I give a harsh laugh. "Really? You're asking *me* that question? Believe me, Elyssia, there's no running away from this shit."

She casts her eyes down. "Crap. Sorry."

I don't understand the whole fae lineage and politics situation, but I do pity her. Nobody likes life out of their control, but she can't help what she's born into any more than a human child.

Elyssia refuses to allow us to support her on the unsteady walk from the car and up the garden path. She fumbles her key in the front door lock and slinks through the door between Ewan and me, the bodyguard more than eager to open the door when they see who's with us. There's no sound in the house, and the solidly built guy with his crew cut hair returns to his seat between the stairs and door, in the large entrance hallway.

I pause, waiting for Portia to appear.

Nothing.

"Portia?" I call. "We're here."

"I'm in the kitchen." I'm surprised by her even tones, as if we've called around for a quick visit. Shouldn't she rush out to see if her daughter is okay?

Elyssia repeats *shit* under her breath the whole way from the hall into the kitchen.

Portia sits at the kitchen island counter with a goldfish-bowl-sized glass in front of her on the granite top. She sips the red wine and appraises her daughter. In contrast, Portia's immaculately dressed and groomed in black slacks and a blue shirt partially open.

"Thank you for returning my daughter."

Neither she nor Elyssia speak to each other. I didn't expect a tender reunion, but I expected more than indifference.

Ewan sets Elyssia's rucksack on the floor, and Portia cranes her neck to see what he has. "Well, there's no point unpacking that."

Elyssia glares at her mother.

"You're leaving tomorrow, darling girl. We agreed you could have another month to spend with your human friends, but you've broken that agreement. I need you gone." Portia gives us a tight smile. "By that I mean away from danger. Where did you find her?"

Now this I've rehearsed. "She was at The Warehouse, living it up with some human friends. I expect she was staying with them."

"I was at La Fee Verte," interrupts Elyssia.

"I do hope you're lying," growls Portia. She climbs down from the stool and approaches her daughter. Portia seizes Elyssa's chin and studies her face. "Is this drugs or alcohol?"

"Magic."

The two stare each other down. Elyssia is definitely her

mother's daughter; I can't imagine they'd ever live together, long term, without a lot of problems.

"You traded your magic?"

Elyssia shrugs and Portia wipes her brow with the back of her hand before turning away. "I suggest you go to your room. Dennis will be outside, should you decide to abscond again. You may've used your magic to slip the last bodyguards you had, but not again. I'll be warding the house."

"Abscond," says Elyssia with a snort. "So polite. So regal. If you make me leave my life here for another court, and I have to marry some dude I don't like, I'll make sure my kingdom is stronger than yours! You'll be sorry you're doing this!"

Whoa. I glance at Ewan and tense, ready for Portia's outburst, a crackle of magic, something.

"Good night, Elyssia," she replies firmly, without looking at her daughter.

I cross my arms, awkward in the silence, a feeling matched by Ewan judging by his gaze at the floor. Man, their world is complicated.

Once Elyssia leaves the room, with her shoulders straight, emulating her mother's haughtiness, Portia pulls out two wine glasses from beneath the bench.

"Join me for a drink."

"No, we need to be getting back to the house," says Ewan.

"And I'm driving," I put in.

Portia ignores us and pours. "How are my favourite boys?"

I blink at her behaving as if we're friends who haven't visited for some time, not estranged allies. "Missing your help right now."

"Mmm?" Portia pushes the glasses towards us and picks

up hers. "Is your Fifth still with you?"

"Yes. And she's not going anywhere," Ewan says in a warning tone.

"So I gather. And how about the delightful War. Is he ready to apologise yet?"

Xander apologise? She knows the likelihood of that, judging by her smirking face.

"If the apology is mutual, I imagine he would," I reply. "Things became a little heated."

Portia carefully cuts cheese and places it onto crackers she has lain out on a plate in front of her, and we wait as she slowly eats. Eventually she licks her fingers and returns her attention our way. "I'm prepared to listen to Xander, if he can agree to my terms."

One thing about Portia, it's impossible to judge what she's thinking. She's clever—putting herself across as a charming and friendly lady—but we've seen her darker moods many times.

"What terms?" asks Ewan. "We'll speak to him."

"An apology. The truth about *everything* you four have done in recent months. Xander must also allow us to question Verity."

I scratch my eyebrow. She certainly likes to pile on her demands.

"And Xander must come to my bed." Another sip, another smile.

"What?" Mine and Ewan's voices reply in shocked unison.

"Xander. Sex. A proof of our unity."

Oh, holy fuck. He would never do something like that. But my shock is joined by a guilty relief that she didn't ask either of us. But of course not, because she perceives Xander as our strongest and the one she needs to conquer.

There's no way anybody could conquer War.

Her laughter chimes around the kitchen. "Your faces! You Pony Boys are so precious! I adore you. I'm joking."

There's a part of me that thinks she isn't. Over the last ten years, Portia's repeatedly propositioned us and then denied she was interested. Is that face saving?

Ewan rubs a hand across his face. "I'm too tired for this, Portia. Can you accept us bringing home Elyssia as a pledge of our loyalty? If we wanted to betray the fae on any level, we wouldn't have helped. We didn't want to interfere because there's enough shit we're dealing with right now, but we did."

"And for that I am very grateful, and yes this does shine a new light on our situation and relationship." She places her fingers on his arm. "I would like to repay your help in some way. Perhaps we could organise to meet, and you can tell me *everything*." She emphasis the word everything.

He looks over at me, and I nod. "As long as you reciprocate with information, Portia, because I think you're holding something back too."

"Of course."

"And I don't want you to bring Logan to the meeting."

Portia drops into one of her silences, the kind where things could go either way. Then she smiles. "I will be in touch tomorrow. I need to attend to my daughter."

She leaves us in the kitchen, where I stare at the school notices attached to the fridge by magnets, at the planner posted on the wall besides Kailey's behaviour chart. The kitchen's filled with the ordinary in the middle of a household that's anything but.

We leave, hearing raised voices above as we pass the stairs, hopeful we may be able to get back on track with Portia and gain some help.

11

JOSS

I stand in the study and cross my arms as I run a gaze along the bookshelves in the quiet room looking for a specific book. The afternoon Vee made it clear our relationship would be between the five of us, and not two, I joked about showing her the pictures in one book, but now I'm concerned this isn't a joke anymore.

The book—containing Truth—is one filled with references to demonic magic, and that scares me. This worried us early on, until we met Vee and discovered how much of us she contained, and how I couldn't sense anything demonic around her. But does her recent behaviour point to a demon connection? Judging by how tricky everything is right now, I'm keeping these worries to myself to avoid an overreaction, especially by Ewan.

Vee's calmer than she was, back to her old self.

I'm not.

I have no fucking idea what I saw when I died, but I'm followed by an unease as great as when the wraith, or whatever the hell it was, followed me. As with the creatures that attacked Ewan, I've spent spare time pouring over books while Ewan looks online.

There's nothing in any mythology that harms in the way the creature killed me. A Horseman. One of the strongest beings on the planet.

But am I? Are we?

What and why did I remember?

The worst part is that the scene loops through my mind. If I drift away, tired by everything, the image of the girls, the gun... death sneak in. Worse still, I find myself in the place I was amongst the screaming. Just thinking about it sets my heart racing at a level that constricts my chest to the point I can't breathe.

I asked Ewan what happened when he died, and he saw nothing. Maybe because he was only dead for minutes?

I'm damn sure Xander or Heath will be targeted next, and if it's Heath... what then? Vee doesn't have the power.

Yet.

"Joss?" Vee's voice pushes through the shadows in my mind and shoves away the memories about to return.

The soft expression and concern in her eyes isn't an emotionless Vee, perhaps Ewan got through to her? The wild-eyed need isn't in her eyes as it was last time we spent time in the study.

Did she really want me that evening? Or was she driven by this primal *something* inside her? Now Vee's calmer about the situation and she hasn't hinted she wants help with eradicating her humanity, I'm relaxing around her. Perhaps I'll discover her true motives.

"I wanted to show you the books. We haven't had time with all the craziness, and that's not disappearing soon, but I think it's important."

"Is this the one with the picture you mentioned? I've been wondering what's so hilarious about that."

I chew on my lip. "It was funny at the time."

As I run a finger along the shelved books to locate the right one, Vee approaches from behind and wraps her arms round my waist. She places her head on my back.

"Are you okay now, Joss?" she says. "You haven't spoken about things fully. You still don't feel right to me."

I loosen her arms and turn, encompassing Vee in mine and pulling her close. She smells good, vanilla-flavoured Vee with her soothing presence. She asked me in the past why I always wanted to hold her when we slept together and always kept amazing self-control. Yeah, that was bloody hard, but I worried if I scared her away, I wouldn't be able to hold her and absorb the comfort she gives that bolsters me when things are tough.

Heath complains how he hates his role as Death; Ewan sometimes barely disguises his stress about the role. Xander? I don't know; his mood swings probably keep him focused in an unfocused way. Me? I crave the closeness, the touch, and the natural comfort from being with somebody who brings out the human Joss and lets me forget the Horseman side.

For me, this is Vee.

"I had a weird vision." I don't mean to say anything; the words spill out.

"When? Just now?"

"No." I sit on the nearby chair, and Vee perches on my

lap, arms wound around my neck. Her easy intimacy draws me closer to her and allows me to admit what I haven't to anybody.

I tell her the story of what I saw the first time and the second. I choke back the words several times, and she grips me tighter smoothing my hair.

I finish, emotionally and physically drained, more than any time I've fought demons—because this time I'm fighting mine. Vee voices what I didn't want her to.

"I know you believe in the Biblical, Joss. Do you think you were in Hell?" Her words are hesitant, spoken into my hair. and I hold her harder.

I swallow. "Yes."

"And do you think the man you saw—"

"Was me?" I interrupt. "Yes."

Vee pulls away and holds my face in both hands. "No. He couldn't be. Joss, you're a good person. You care. You're intuitive. The day I arrived in your lives, you helped me. You never showed a single sign of malice."

I pull her hand from my cheek, and every question that's come to me when I've lain in the dark spills out. "But what if the person I saw in the two visions is another me, and I was in Hell because of the things I did to people? What if this is my second chance, and if I fuck up, I'm dragged back to Hell? I'm worried that's what happened to the Horsemen who came before us."

My anxiety rises as concern flickers across Vee's face. My words sound too convincing.

"But we can't be sure Hell exists, Joss."

I gesture at the books. "Something does. Maybe under a different name, not labelled by a religion. I've said this before. I call him Lucifer for want of a better name."

"Call who, Joss?"

"Whoever rules the realm beyond the portal the Order want to breech. The one who plans to send through his demon race to conquer the human world. What if all this shit happening is to prevent us paying attention to the portals? We're distracted."

Vee chews her lip. "How do you know if the portals are under threat from those on the other side?"

"We sense it."

"And do you now?"

"No."

"Then don't worry. Focus on what's happening."

We fall into silence, and I fight the quickened breathing that betrays my fear. I need to know more.

"I thought you were quiet because you were recovering from the attack. I didn't know this was happening."

"I can't stop thinking about it, Vee. I doubt myself. I'm terrified I'm going to lapse back into whoever *he* was."

"*He* wasn't you, Joss. This is who you are. The man who loves and cares for us all. The guy who succeeded in resisting my request to lose part of who I am because of that love and loyalty."

I look into Vee's eyes, seeking a true answer to my next question, even though I know she can't lie. "Do you still want that, Vee? Do you still want to lose your human side?"

She looks away, stroking my cheek with her thumb lost in thought. "Sometimes." She looks back. "I fight it. Ewan made me realise what would happen if I do. I want to love you all, and be loved by you all. I want the closeness we have as five, and all that's happening is I'm pushing you away."

I catch a hint of something else. "But?"

"But there's something here." Vee places a fist on her chest. "Something gnawing I can't explain, and I'm scared it will devour me."

We share a look, an understanding. Do we all have the same thing eating at us? I rub her legs. "Let me show you the book. Maybe that will explain something—to both of us."

The blue leather-bound book smells of the past, the pages musty to join the peculiar smell the combined ageing books give the room. Every book was in this room when we arrived, as if left there for research. I found this one a few months later; it took me a while to work through them. Many confused me with their rows and rows of scrawled text in an unfamiliar language. This one included images, and I was drawn to the contents as I began to recognise and decipher things.

I open at the beginning, a blank page of thick paper.

"This starts with Biblical stories, a history lesson, I guess." I flick past pages crammed with neatly printed text. "These are Biblical verses about us."

Vee scratches her head. "About the Biblical Horsemen."

I nod. "You should read this, if you don't know our namesakes' full story. Even these days, humans predict the seven seals will open into an apocalypse. We only know of six portals, so maybe one has already. But we're supposed to walk through and devastate the world, so this obviously isn't accurate as we didn't."

"Okay. So what else?"

I flick through pages until I find illustrations. "These show where the portals are located. There's one on each continent."

"Wow. What if they were all attacked at once? There're four of you and you're in one place."

"Yeah, we asked ourselves that question." I point at the page, showing lines running between the portal symbols. "I think they're linked, as if they need to be opened in a specific order."

"And have any been breached while you've been in the world?"

"No. We've visited them to inspect what they are, but that's it. Our main concern is keeping what's already here under control to stop any attack on them from this side."

"And you think that's what's happening now?"

"I don't know. I suspect there's a more coordinated plot that involves taking us out first."

I continue turning the pages, and Vee leans over as the Horsemen's names appear on separate pages, with visual representations of our powers. She laughs. "Was this a training guide?"

I give a wry smile. "If it is, we didn't find the book until after our powers triggered."

"I bet that was a shock!"

"Oh yeah. Instinct ruled in those situations." I scratch my nose and turn a page. "Here's you."

A simple depiction of a female figure surrounded by four males, carefully inked in black, is drawn on the page. Beneath, a simple diagram of a circle represents Vee and four lines representing us touching the circle, two at the top, two at the bottom.

"So there's Truth at the centre of us."

Vee studies this for a minute.

"Xander originally thought the four of us combined created Truth, but we gradually became aware Truth was another entity. Partly because of this." On the next page, a more anatomically correct version of a woman graces the page.

Vee snorts. "Oh, nice. I think they captured my likeness well, though I think my breasts are smaller than that."

I chuckle. "I'll check and confirm later, if you like?"

She flicks my nose and kisses me.

"So, the next page?"

Vee goes to turn the page, and I place my hand on it. "That's everything relevant in the book."

"Liar." She pushes my hand away and picks up the book, then rests it on her lap.

I sigh. "Just don't think this is anything more than a symbolic representation. Like the circle and lines."

"Whoa!" Page turned, Vee almost drops the book. "What the hell?"

Yeah, the picture I was going to show as a joke, days ago, when she spoke about wanting us all. I intended to use this to tease Xander, who was adamant he had no connection to her.

On the page are the five figures represented throughout the book. Joined.

Physically.

"Well that's a bit bloody different to the circles and lines!" Vee continues to stare, brow pinched. She points. "Is this suggesting we'll do... *this*?"

"Uh. I don't know. I think it just illustrates what we thought. That Truth is a central part of the Four Horsemen. That a Fifth is part of us."

"But together? At the same time?"

I watch warily, attempting to pick up on her emotions.

Then she laughs.

"Omigod, what did Xander think about this once he realised Truth was a woman, and this depicted him having group sex with his brother involved?" She snorts a laugh, but I can't help smiling too.

"What do you think?" I ask cautiously.

She taps the page. "What do I think about having sex with you all at once? Seriously, Joss?"

"No! I mean what do you think it means?"

"Probably what you said. This situation won't happen, by the way, even if you were all willing." She laughs again. "Oh, man... I wouldn't know what to do with you all."

I share her amusement, and a relief Vee doesn't believe this is any more than symbolic. The idea does not appeal to me either. At all.

"Yes. The other symbol, the circle and lines, is just a physical representation of that. Confirms what we think, right? That if I have sex with all of you, I'll become stronger." She shakes her head with another chuckle. "Just individually though."

I nod and ignore the Ewan-shaped elephant in the room. "Yes. There's something on the next page that's weird."

Vee flips over. The next page is blank. "What?"

"Huh?" I pull the book from her and stare down. "There are two pages missing. I think; I'm sure I remember a page with symbols on. I was going to compare them to the Collector's book." I rub my head. Did I imagine it? I've studied a lot of books recently. "Maybe it was a different book." I run a finger along where the pages bind, but there's no sign anything was torn out. "It was another figure. This was who we thought was trying to get through, the one the demons tell us about."

"I could help you check other books?" suggests Vee as she sets the one she's holding on the table.

I rub my face. "Sure. Another time. I'm exhausted after tonight."

"Hmm. Yes. Elyssia. Do you think this will help mend things with Portia?"

"I hope so." I wrap my arm around Vee's waist and look up at her. There's a troubled look in her eyes as she looks back. "Are *you* okay? Is this about the book?"

She touches my lip with two fingers. "I'm sorry about

what happened last time we were in here. I shouldn't have pressured you like I did."

I laugh in disbelief. "Are you talking about the sex, Vee? Believe me, you didn't pressure me into that. I always told you I was just waiting for the go ahead."

"No, I mean trying to make you take my emotions, putting you in that position."

I pull her head towards me and rest my forehead against hers. "Honestly, the only position I was thinking about was the one I was in with you."

"Very funny."

"Seriously, I wouldn't have done that if I thought there was any chance I would lose control and do what you'd wanted. I care too much about the girl I'm holding now to risk losing her."

Vee presses her soft lips against mine, and we hold our mouths together with the humming emotion passing between us. "I don't want you to think I was just seducing you because my powers took over."

"I know," I run a finger along her cheek. "I can tell how you really feel, remember."

Sighing, Vee wraps her arms around my neck. "Thank you."

I slide a hand beneath Vee's shirt and stroke her warm skin. "But you do realise I'll never be able to sit in this study again without picturing you naked on the desk."

In this moment, a peace and happiness washes over me that I haven't felt for days. Vee's. She climbs from my knee and holds out a hand. "Let's go to bed."

I arch a brow. "Are you seducing me again, Miss Verity?"

Laughing, she pulls at my arm. "No. I want you to seduce me."

Not a problem.

Never a problem.

"And I can show you how much I care," she whispers. "And that I'm Vee, and I want her to stay."

12

*V*EE

A meeting with Portia summons images of audiences in her craft room. Maybe a visit to wherever she holds court with her fae council. I'm surprised she'd choose the local community centre in the middle of town, but not surprised to hear she's involved with amateur dramatics.

We park outside the single-storey, red brick building, and the six of us walk through the blustery weather into the foyer. The place smells of floor polish and stale food; notices pinned to a large board advertise parents' groups and the play due to perform in a few weeks' time: Macbeth.

Joss taps it. "Shakespeare, huh? Who do you think Portia's playing?"

"The starring role, of course," replies Heath.

Our footsteps echo as we walk to the main hall. People pass in the opposite direction, chatting in pairs and holding scripts, walking from the hall's direction. Actors and actresses from Portia's play? We step to one side to allow them to pass, the guys naturally receiving a few double takes from girls who look straight through me.

Chairs are stacked along the wall in the large hall, and Portia sits on the small stage at one end of the room, chatting to another woman who I don't recognise. A tall man in jeans and a black shirt sits a few metres away and stands as we approach. Portia looks up to see why her bodyguard stood to alert and waves a hand at him to sit.

"I know them." She checks her phone before turning her attention our way. "You're a little early."

"'Ill met by moonlight, proud Titania,'" announces Joss in a theatrical style.

She scowls at him. "Wrong play."

I look to him in confusion and he explains, "'A Midsummer Night's Dream', it's a play about—"

"Fairies," Portia interrupts. "Very funny."

"Joss, don't upset her," says Xander in a low voice.

He shakes his head in amusement. "Sure, Xander. I'll follow your diplomatic style."

Portia approaches. "Who's this?" She points at Seth with her well-thumbed script.

"Seth Marks," he says and holds his hand out. "Nice to meet you."

"No, I mean, *who* are you."

"A friend of Vee's," he offers.

Portia pulls a face and looks at Heath. "He's a little different to you all. Why are you with somebody more... *normal*?"

Heath glances at Portia's friend who's carefully weighing up the guys. Trying to decide who I'm with? Waiting for a look or smile?

"Long story," Heath replies.

"And one I'm sure you'll tell me." She leans to one side to look past him, where Xander stands at the edge of our group, silently measuring his next words, I hope.

"How are you, Xander?" she asks, saccharin sweet.

"Keen to work on solving our problems," he replies in an even tone.

The tension between the two radiates. "And do you have anything you wish to say to me?"

Xander looks back, impassive.

"Do you have somewhere we can sit and talk?" interrupts Joss.

Portia stands and brushes dust from her yoga pants. "We can use the meeting room by the kitchen."

The woman with her finally speaks. "I should be going."

"Oh, I apologise. I never introduced you. These are some acquaintances of mine." Portia introduces us one by one. The guys nod politely but are disinterested and distracted. I close my eyes hoping she doesn't call them by her pet name for the group, especially not in front of a tense Xander.

"Will you be coming to watch the play?" Portia asks. "I'm sure we can find you an invite to the after party."

Ewan stares at her as if she just asked him to supervise another children's Halloween party. "Not my scene."

"Oh, I'm sure the others would love to come. They really don't have enough fun." Portia cocks an expectant eyebrow. "Wouldn't you?"

Why the hell does Portia need to start with the power play already?

"Maybe Joss," replies Ewan. "He likes Shakespeare if he can quote it."

"Maybe I will." Joss inclines his head. "Could we talk now?"

"I'll watch. I'd like an evening out." Everybody stares at Seth.

Portia breaks into a huge smile. "Thank you. I'll let you know when tickets are on sale."

Omigod. I cannot believe that in the middle of all the crap swirling around us, we are standing in a community centre discussing bloody amateur dramatics. Xander shares my thoughts, judging by his thinning lips and crossed arms.

"Where's this room?" He points at the double doors to our right. "This way?"

We're forced to continue waiting as Portia arranges a meet up with her thespian friend and leaves her with air kisses.

"Such a lovely girl," Portia says as she watches her leave.

Portia leads us to a door opposite the hallway entrance and into a small room with a table and chairs. Previous occupants have left pens and papers on the table, which Seth gathers into a pile.

"Be a darling and make some drinks, Verity," Portia says as she sits. "The kitchen's along the hall. First door. You can't miss it. I'd love a tea."

I bite inside my cheek to prevent a retort. Again. This woman does *not* like me.

"I'm good, thanks," mutters Xander and everybody but Seth declines.

"I'll help," says Joss. "I'm better at making tea anyway."

With a wink, he guides me from the room before anybody else can speak, and I glance back at a Seth who sits beside Heath clutching the manilla folder he brought.

"Are you okay?" Joss asks as we head into the small kitchen space. "You're quiet today."

"Portia," I reply in a low voice. "I don't care that she

doesn't like or trust me, but her passive aggression and attempts to belittle me are annoying."

"She's just jealous, Vee," he replies and strokes hair from my face. "Apart from the fact you're more powerful than her, you're smoking hot and have the Horsemen doing what she'd like to do."

"Which is?"

He arches a brow. "Anything you ask. If she knew you'd slept with more than one of us she'd be insanely jealous."

I attempt to hide my smug and fail as Joss laughs at me and curls a hand around my waist. "She's not used to being outshone."

"I bet. So her attitude isn't only because she believes Logan's opinion of me?"

"No. If she believed him, she wouldn't be here."

Carrying a tray filled with mugs, we walk past the bodyguard now stationed outside the meeting room, and I hand him the drink he asked for. Few school mums have a protective detail; how does Portia explain his presence? He's younger and attractive despite his surly look. How many rumours exist about her relationship with this man? Because I bet she has one.

The others sit in the room, in silence, which doesn't bode well. Portia taps a message on her phone ignoring them, and Seth sits bolt upright, file now on the table in front.

"Thank you, sweetheart," says Portia as I set down her mug. She wipes the rim with her thumb and sips. If she says one word about the quality, I'll be the one causing diplomatic issues.

"Now. What should we talk about?" she asks.

"How's Elyssia?" asks Ewan.

"Safe. Thank you." I bet that thank you almost choked her.

"You're welcome," replies Heath. "As I said last night, I hope this helps mend some of the division between us."

Portia's eyes bore into Xander's face, who continues his taciturn attitude to the situation. Earlier, Heath gave his brother a run down on what to say, and what not to say, and for once he bows to the consensus he needs to apologise. One thing I'm sure of is this apology will choke him too.

"I'm sorry for my behaviour the other night," he says, and they train their gaze on each other.

"And I'm sorry that things became such a difficult situation," Portia replies.

The guys told me how difficult it is to regain friendship with the grudge-holding race, and that Portia's decision to give them another chance indicates Portia's hiding how much she needs their help.

"We shall move on and prove to each other that our relationship is mutually beneficial," Portia continues.

Heath's stiff shoulders relax, and he rests back in the chair. "Thank you."

"Now, explain who Seth is." She graces him with a smile and he smiles back, smoothing his hands over the folder.

"Seth's someone who's been collecting information about suspicious activity that he's prepared to share."

"And you can trust him?" she asks.

"As much as we can trust anybody," replies Xander and clamps his mouth shut at Heath's stern look.

Over the next ten minutes, Ewan explains the events from the last few days: the murders, the creatures, Seth and Casey, and suspicions about Nova Pharm. Portia listens without a word, face impassive, blinking in places, such as when the Collector's name is mentioned.

"Do you have photographs of these runes?" she asks.

Xander pulls out his phone and slides it across the table towards her. She purses her lips as she studies. "I have no idea what they are. Sorry."

"We didn't expect you to," replies Ewan. "Even the Collector couldn't identify them."

"The Collector isn't known to be helpful." Her face sours. "Good luck in acquiring *his* help."

"Do you know anybody who works at Nova Pharm?" asks Heath. "I met a fae there. Kai Fielding. Do you know him?"

"Not personally, no. I'm really not au fait with every workplace my subjects are employed at."

I almost choke on my tea at her calling them subjects, but she's a queen, of course they are.

Heath slides a printed sheet, from Seth's file, across the table to Portia. "We've identified as many names as we can, but there are some we don't recognise. We thought you may know some from your connections."

She scans the document. "There aren't any important fae named here, or any we have any suspicions about. I think you need to look elsewhere for your perpetrators."

"Hang on," says Xander. "What do you mean suspicions? Have you discovered people within your court you suspect, since we last spoke?"

"There are some we watch. Younger fae in particular, which is another reason I want Elyssia away from all this. I believe she'll endanger herself."

Heath taps the paper. "This guy. Have you heard of him?"

"He's new on the scene," puts in Seth. "I think because the board know we're onto them, they've enlisted someone else."

Xander turns a frown to Seth. He never told us this.

"'Onto them,'" repeats Portia, amused by the turn of

phrase. She runs a long finger down the sheet, stops and taps with her nail.

"Alasdair Faulkner? Are you sure?"

Xander leans forward, elbows on the table. "You know him?"

"He's human, and I've been to his events in the past. He throws wonderful parties. Haven't you heard of him?"

"No, or we wouldn't be asking." I shake my head at Xander. "Thanks for offering to help," he adds gruffly.

"I didn't realise he was connected to Nova Pharm. He's from old money and doesn't need to work. He bought an estate in Scotland, and now he pretends he's laird. A little of a party boy too, shall we say?"

"Have you heard of the Myriad Foundation?" asks Seth. "He's involved, we think."

Portia's brow furrows. "He did mention he was thinking about using his money more beneficially, but I don't know the charity name. Is this relevant?"

"Fundraising for what?" asks Heath.

"He's planning to work with drug addicts, and ex-addicts, to help them find employment and housing. Quite the benefactor. I think he's setting up a rehab facility on part of his estate in Scotland."

Xander's sullen look lifts. "Do you know how he's raising funds for this? How well do you know him? Do you have details?"

"So many questions, Xander! He's approached businesses for sponsorship, including Paul's. My human husband spends a lot of time networking, and Alasdair is planning a launch where businesses donate to charity, and they have the chance to spend a weekend on his estate networking. Also to see where their money will be going, of course. A win-win, should we say."

"Are you going?" asks Heath.

She pulls a face. "No. Why would I want to spend a weekend surrounded by humans I have no real connection to?"

"Is anybody you know going?" presses Heath.

"No. We were invited, but..." She wrinkles her nose. "I like his parties, but a whole weekend... No thank you."

Xander blows air into his cheeks. "Do you have enough of a connection to get us an invite? If one of your husbands was invited, and yourself, can we be your company representatives?"

Portia laughs and then her mouth forms into an O. "Are you serious?"

"I bloody hope not," replies Ewan.

Heath tucks the paper back into the folder. "I think it's a good idea. There's no headquarters for this charity yet, and we can't exactly break into his house to see what we can find. An estate like that will be crawling with security."

Ewan balks. "You're suggesting a whole weekend with humans stuck where?"

"Scotland."

"I've never been to Scotland." Seth sips his tea. "Might be nice."

Ewan's unamused look grows. "What? Would he come?"

"He doesn't leave our sight, remember?" says Xander.

Portia tips her head. "Why?"

"Umm. Because of the threat to his life." Heath and Xander glance at each other.

"I don't mind. I quite like the idea," Seth continues.

"I thought you liked people about as much as we do?" asks Ewan sarcastically.

"You forget how many months I spent investigating this

shit. Don't you think I'd like an opportunity to follow up on the lead too?"

"I bet most companies aren't sending six delegates!" retorts Ewan. "Leave me behind, please."

"Not happening," replies Xander. "We stick together."

"Ewan is correct. I can't ask Paul to send too many delegates." Portia sets down her mug. "However, the weekend includes partners too so we can work with that. Six of you will be an ideal number."

"What the hell?" asks Ewan.

"I know Vee doesn't like to choose, but maybe she can pretend, just for a day or two. The rest of you can do the same—with each other."

No. Hell, no.

Xander's eyes widen. "Are you suggesting we pretend to be partners? Like, in a relationship?"

Joss chuckles, but none of the other guys shares his amusement. "Can I have Heath, please? The rest of you snore."

"No way." Xander crosses his arms.

"Why? Do you have a problem with same-sex relationships?" Portia asks.

"I couldn't give a crap about anybody's relationships, or what they do. But there is no way I can pretend to be with Ewan and definitely not Seth!"

"Hey! You can't presume Vee wants to pretend you're exclusive," protests Heath. "Besides, you won't fool anyone since you're always fighting. What if she punches you in the face again?"

Xander involuntarily touches his cheek.

"I didn't punch him," I retort.

Portia's smug amusement riles me. "Vee is attacking you, Xander?"

Before he can respond, Joss interrupts. "You and Vee? So that leaves Seth with Ewan! Oh, man."

I sit forward. "Excuse me? Don't I get a say in this?"

Portia sighs. "I haven't promised I can do this for you yet. If I do organise it though, it will be three company representatives and their partners." She pulls out her phone. "Plus, I have a favour to ask in return. I'd like you to deal with this person."

She places the phone on the table, and Heath slides it over to look. "Deal with Mac? If humans aren't threatened, we don't touch anybody. We're not mercenaries."

"Yes. Mac, the man with no surname who violated my daughter."

"Oh, no way. We're not getting involved in this shit. If you have an issue with anybody from that club, get it shut down," Ewan replies.

"I don't want my name connected to anything that could cause trouble."

"No." Xander's response is firm, final.

"Then I can't help you."

"How many times, Portia?" Xander's tone fills with exasperation, not anger. "This shit affects the fae too. Not helping us could put you in more danger."

She jabs a finger at the screen. "My daughter is in danger."

Heath rests his elbows on the table and rubs both hands down his face, swearing.

"We could ask Syv or Abel to sort it?" suggests Seth.

"Excuse me?" Portia narrows her eyes at the guys. "Is your little friend telling me you're involved with that half-demon bitch?" I cringe as her voice rises. "Do you know what she stole from us and how important it was?"

"Nice one, Seth," mutters Heath. "Thanks, mate."

I feel like putting my head in my hands too. So much politics, it's insane.

"I knew it!" She points a finger at Xander. "Someone told me you'd asked her to help you before, and I didn't want to believe them."

"When?" asks Heath, sharply.

"A couple of weeks before *she* arrived."

"*She* has a name," I say in a low voice.

I don't miss Ewan's "we're going to talk about this look" to Xander. He was involved with Syv before now? No secrets, huh? Hypocrite.

"Verity." Portia smiles. "You seem different since I last saw you. More powerful. Do you feel more powerful?"

I hold her challenge, ignoring the undertones. "I feel I'm becoming more who I need to be."

"And what's that?"

"Part of the guys."

She gives a seductive bite to her lip and looks at Xander. "Has she claimed you all as I suspected she would, or left any of you for me?"

Xander huffs. "You're relentless, Portia."

"I'm used to getting what I want, that's all." She twirls the mug on the table in front of her. "Surely one girl isn't enough to satisfy all your... urges."

Oh, good God.

"Some things are more important than sex," says Ewan gruffly. "Will you help us or not?"

She taps her phone screen. "Once you've dealt with him, yes. I'm sure if you dig deep enough you'll find there are humans sneaking into the club, and you could *punish* him for that."

Ewan rubs his mouth and looks at Heath.

"I don't care what reason you give. Eliminate him so I don't cause problems by doing it myself."

The conversation deadens, each person in the room preoccupied by their own thoughts. I'm most interested in what Xander's are, whether he'll agree, and where we go from here.

13

*H*EATH

*L*a Fee Verte operates 24/7, but with less patrons in the daytime. Inside, some sit beneath the violet lights at the bar, drinking, and a few sit in shadowy corners holding meetings. I'd love to know exactly what about.

Most come for their magic fix.

Xander and me attract attention when we walk in. War and Death paying the place a visit? Everybody knows we're not just here for a drink.

I study the people around, the obvious addicts and the deadbeats who slump over their drinks. Many shift their gazes away from me. Because I'm Death or because they've something to hide?

I'm unsurprised when I spot Syv at the bar, chatting to the blue-haired barman. She makes sweeping gestures in the air as she does and is the most animated person in here.

Xander wanders over to talk to her while I watch the door and stairs in case Mac appears, or bolts out the entrance.

"Has she found anything connected to the rune yet?" I ask Xander when he returns.

He shakes his head. "I asked if Mac was around, and the barman said he's upstairs."

"Wow, way to sell out your friends."

"The guy knows better than to lie to me. Everybody in this joint knows not to cross us, because I bet everybody here has something they'd rather we didn't know about."

He's right. I look over, and Syv gives a small wave before returning to her drink and chat.

"I told her about our deal with Portia."

"Xander! Maybe you should've asked Syv to sort the situation. I don't like this."

A skinny guy in leather and a half-shredded black vest passes with an empty glass, and determination, as he approaches the bar. Xander lowers his voice. "I don't think we need to kill Mac. I'll give him the chance to get the hell out of here and the country."

I rub my temples. "Portia has asked us to do this. What if she finds out we didn't fulfil our end of the bargain?"

"If she doesn't find out until after our visit to Alasdair, I'm fine. After that... I'll deal with the situation if she discovers the truth later."

That's what I'm worried about.

"Seriously, Heath. I'm surprised Mac's still here. Sure, these guys have nothing to do with Portia's fae, but they know how powerful she is. The owner won't be happy Mac's drawn attention to the place." He gestures to the stairs. "C'mon, I'm not hanging around."

We tread up the narrow staircases, past the room we sat in before with the others, which is dark and empty today.

There's no music and nobody dancing in the other rooms, the place a shell of the normal place, as the many people here are shells of themselves.

We reach the top floor. A guy sits on a chair outside Mac's room, staring at the carpet as he jiggles his legs. His long black hair sweeps forward, obscuring his face, and he picks at the chair edge.

Mac's client looks up when he hears our footsteps. Purer fae's faces are sculpted into sharp features with a strange beauty, but this fae's high cheek bones protrude in his sunken skin.

He regards us with dulled violet eyes surrounded by dark circles. "I'm next."

Xander doesn't respond.

"Is Mac in there?" I ask.

"He went into the room just after I arrived. I've been waiting ten minutes. He's late."

I glance at Xander, who immediately tries the door handle. He rattles, and movement sounds in the room behind; a door slams.

"There's a window in his bedroom," I say to Xander. "I saw when we found Elyssia."

"Fuck." In usual Xander style, he kicks at the door.

The other guy jumps to his feet and wraps arms around himself. "Whoa, dude. Mac won't like that; he hates interruptions."

Ignoring him, Xander kicks the door again. The chair someone pushed beneath the handle, in an attempt to stop anybody opening the door, cracks under the force. I follow as Xander strides into the room. The place looks the same as when I last walked in on Mac, swapping magic with the girl. This time the chair's broken on the floor and the door to the room we found Elyssia in is open.

Xander rushes in. "Shit! The fucker left."

I peer into the room after him. Clothes cover the bed; discarded items are strewn on the floor. There's no sign of a struggle; this is someone trying to decide what to take in a hurry.

"Do you think we heard Mac leaving?"

Xander crosses the bedroom to a dirty open window and leans out. "I'm bloody sure it was. He could've gone this way."

Beneath the window, there's a lower floor's flat roof between this room and the ground, but still a long drop as this is the third floor in a tall building.

"I reckon Mac's always planned this as an escape route, and not just from us." More of Xander's figure disappears through the window as he surveys the area. "There's a skip close enough to jump onto."

I join him at the window. The back entrance to the club is below us, and there's no sight or sound of anybody in the dirty alleyway between this building and those opposite. In the daylight, the guy won't be able to hide long.

"You think he just left?" I ask.

"I wanna know who told him we were here!" Xander climbs from the window, boots thudding as he lands on the roof below. "He won't be far."

I watch as Xander effortlessly climbs down, jumping from roof, to skip, to the ground, and I sigh before following. When I land, I trip and almost end up in a soggy cardboard box. The stench of rotting food turns my stomach, and I cover my nose with a sleeve.

One end of the alleyway stops at a brick-walled dead end; the other leads out onto a main street. Voices and the clatter of pans and utensils sound from the open door at a nearby cafe's kitchen. Xander points. "You check in there. I'll search around. We would've seen Mac if he ran the other way. He didn't get much of a head start."

I unsheathe the knife inside my jacket and stride into the hot kitchen and a tempting aroma of Thai spices mixed in the steam. A stout man in a chef's white clothes halts in his work and stares at me.

"Did a guy walk in here?" I ask.

The other man pauses from chopping vegetables and vigorously shakes his head as he eyes my weapon, gripping his knife too. "No, sir."

"Are you sure?" I point the knife in his direction. "You'd better not be lying."

He backs up, fear filling his features and the knife shaking in his hands. I take a quick scout around the small kitchen, but there's nowhere large enough to hide between the metal units and stovetops.

"Did he go through there?" I point at the double doors leading through to the cafe.

"No. Nobody came here."

Years of this shit and reading people tell me he isn't lying, but I need to check regardless.

I shove open the double doors between the kitchen and the cafe and walk into a room crammed with tables, chairs, and surprised people. The sedate mood drops, replaced by panic when they see Death joining them for coffee. A woman half screams as she notices my knife and grabs her toddler from the stroller beside her. A man at the nearest table jumps to his feet and steps toward me.

"Crap. Sorry." I push the knife back into my jacket and hold my hands up. "I'm looking for someone."

Before the stunned customers turn on me, I back up. Clashes with humans are not a good idea. Then I pause. No. He may've run through the front.

I navigate my way around the tables and open the door with my shoulder. If Mac came out this way, he's disappeared because there's no sign of anybody outside.

"Excuse me," I mutter on my way back into the cafe and run back through the double doors before the man considering whether to tackle me tries. The guys in the kitchen haven't moved, and I throw them a look on the way past before I burst back into the rear alley.

"Xander?" The alleyway is empty, and I stride along to check between skips and behind boxes.

I hear a scuffle and a growling voice nearby, to my left behind piled refuse.

Xander.

I creep around the pile, hand on my knife hilt, and come across a dark, narrow passage between two buildings that leads between the front and rear alleyways. The space is barely wide enough for both Xander and a dishevelled Mac. He's swapped his smart suit for dirty jeans and a heavy jacket, and has a rucksack at his feet.

Xander holds the point of his knife in front of Mac's throat, who has his hands up in a gesture of surrender. I block the exit and wait for a signal from Xander what to do.

"No, no!" Mac flattens himself against the wall. "Listen." He pants. "I have information."

Xander's stance slackens slightly. "Information about what?"

"The shit that's happening to you. I see and hear things, yeah?"

Xander presses the point against Mac's skin. "What things? I thought you and your fucked-up mates didn't get involved."

"Wrong." He stares back. "Some of my 'fucked-up mates'

hear things too. And we know about the threat to Portia and about your Fifth and the trouble she's causing."

"Everybody knows this, I'm sure," snaps Xander. He presses the tip closer, and it nicks Mac's skin.

He chokes back a laugh. "Did you know some of her closest are working with the Order now?"

"What?" I ask. "Who?"

Mac stares between us, eyes wild. "I'll tell you if you agree to let me go." He wipes at the perspiration on his forehead.

"If you have any useful information, yeah, we will. But you need to get far away from here. I suggest the fucking Antarctic."

Mac pushes at Xander's arm to move the knife from his throat. "Okay. I have fae clients who want the magic I take from the kids. I sell the power for a pretty penny."

"How?" I ask.

"Easy. I transfer the magic to these clients the way the others do to me. Then they pay me a shit load to keep quiet."

Xander drops his arm. "Name them. Important fae?"

Mac swallows and touches his neck where the knife cut him. "You can guarantee my safety, right?"

"Uh. No. But we can give you a head start."

"Well, let's start with her adviser's husband. Logan? Heard of him?"

Holy fuck. I knew it.

"Yeah, we're aware of him."

"He's not someone I trade with directly, but I've heard his name. I'm certain shit's going down inside their perfect world." He laughs. "They're no better than us, but at least I know who my enemies are."

Xander leans closer. "Tell me everything you've heard about Logan."

"As far as I know, Logan's linked to the fae who are buying my magic to strengthen themselves. I guess he can't enlist fae at his powerful level, so he's recruiting from the bottom and helping them gain stronger magic."

"Holy shit," I mutter. "I thought he was one of Portia's closest."

"How do you know all this?" demands Xander.

"Uh. When people are stoned, I ask questions and they tell me anything. It's always good to have some dirt on people in case I need to get myself out of situations like this, right?"

"Smart guy," snarls Xander.

"Yeah, so if you let me go, you'll understand why I'm getting the fuck out of here. What do you think'll happen if anyone discovers I opened my mouth?"

I drag my hands through my hair, watching Xander. He's pissed off and fired up; that isn't unusual or difficult to see, but can he keep calm?

I step forward. "Is Logan working with the Order?"

"No clue." Xander pushes the knife at Mac again. "Seriously, man. I don't know! I don't even know why he's doing this shit. Maybe they're pissed off with Portia treating them like she's a goddess not a queen. They say the woman behaves like she's this untouchable who calls the shots. I guess they want her out."

"Why the hell would fae want to become involved with the Order?" I ask Xander. "That makes no sense."

"Demon claws in society," he replies, eyes still on Mac. "Logan has to be involved. Why else divide us from Portia? Who else could bring a demon close enough to assassinate her, unless he was high up in her court?"

"We need to let her know," I say.

"We've no proof Logan's involved. This could cause more

crap between us. Talk about it later."

Mac sucks in a breath. "Listen. Can you just let me go? Seriously, I'll get out of here, and nobody will see anything of me again."

Xander places a hand on Mac's chest and looks around at me. We both know that's doubtful; disappearing in the supernatural world isn't easy.

"Do you have allies?" I ask. "Someone who'll help you. And how do I know you won't run to Logan and tell them about us?"

He pauses. "Because people have already crossed him and not survived. My chances are better if I keep away from a mind-reading, powerful fae who's big mates with demons."

"This is insane," I mutter under my breath.

"So?" Xander looks to me. "Let him go? Or not? I reckon a cleaner death by one of us would be better than what he could suffer at the hands of others."

"No! Guys, come on!"

The smug dealer we dealt with the other night when looking for Elyssia isn't so cocky now. I sense his self-preservation would stop him going to anybody else.

"Xan, if you let him go and Portia finds out, we're in trouble."

"He's dead anyway," Xander says to me in a flat voice. "There's no way he'll come out of this situation in one piece."

"You'll let me take my chances, right?" He turns a pleading look to Xander. "*Right*?"

"Okay. One more thing. Where do they meet? Who's in charge?"

"C'mon, dude," he continues to plead. "I don't know that or I'd tell you!" Xander's eyes narrow, and he doesn't move an inch. "Seriously, I know I won't be able to hide from you guys. I'm not going to do anything to piss you off!"

Xander finally steps back. "I'm giving you a chance, Mac. I shouldn't but I'm feeling generous. But if I find you anywhere near this place or city again, I won't hesitate to kill you. Understood?"

Mac slides to the floor and grabs his rucksack handle, enthusing his thanks over and over. Xander leaves him where he is with a reminder what'll happen if he doesn't leave the area, then takes my arm and guides me to the edge of the passageway.

I frown when Xander pulls us behind the skip. "We wait here. I have a feeling about something."

I've no clue why Xander wants us hidden behind a skip, but sometimes his ideas and methods make no sense. Five minutes standing in the cold, feeling my feet numb, and I'm fed up.

"Let's go," I complain.

"Nope. We watch him leave."

A figure steps from the passageway with his rucksack over one shoulder. Mac bows his head and yanks his jacket hood up to obscure his face. He hunches over and slinks along the alley without looking around, before disappearing at a faster pace around the corner onto the street.

Xander huffs. "Okay. Nobody else is nearby."

A solitary snowflake drifts onto my sleeve, and I turn my head to the sky. Another flake drops onto my nose, and I wipe it away. The strange stillness that precedes a snowfall fills the sky white-grey as the final step into winter begins.

"Let's head home," I say and yank my hood hard against my head.

We tread away through the snow already dusting the ground, away from La Fee Verte and from another puzzle piece we're unsure how it fits.

Slowly but surely things are adding up.

14

---

*X*ANDER

*T*he snow falls thicker as we drive back to the
house and settles on the ground. By the time we
reach home, the surroundings are blanketed in white, but at
least the snowstorm stopped short of creating drifts. I hope
the weather doesn't get any bloody worse, because if all goes
to plan, we're headed to Scotland in a couple of days. The
last thing I need is blocked roads interfering in our plans.

Portia permitting.

Mac's news adds another layer, and things are becoming
clearer. This has to be a new alliance between a fae element
and the Order. Why, though? Do they know something we
don't? I can't imagine hatred of Portia would be enough to
forge a new bond with their sworn enemies, which indicates
the Order could be closer than we realise to getting what
they want: portals open and the big guy and his army
through.

This leaves two unknowns. How far they are with their plans, and exactly what waits on the other side. In the past, the Order taunted us that we have no chance against whoever he is. Joss holds onto his theory this is Lucifer, and there's a Biblical connection, otherwise why our names? I'm not sold on that idea, but whoever or whatever waits to break through is powerful enough to devastate the world, otherwise why would our job involve protecting portals?

"Are you okay, Xander?"

I blink around at Heath, unaware I've sat in the car outside the house without speaking. "Yeah. My mind's on overdrive, that's all."

"What do we do about Logan and Portia?"

"We tell the other guys and see what they think, but I'm cautious about saying anything without proof. I don't want to cause another shitstorm with the fae."

Heath rubs a hand across his mouth and stares ahead into the grey afternoon.

"But not Seth, Heath. I don't want him to know anything about this. It's bad enough he was there when she asked us to kill him. As far as he's concerned, we've done what Portia asked."

"Might keep him on his toes."

"Exactly." I open the car door. "I'm happy for him to keep thinking we'll take out our enemies."

Our feet crunch across the snow, spoiling the perfect white pathway. "I'm inclined to agree with you about Logan and not saying anything to Portia yet."

"Good. That'll help. Joss will probably disagree, but at this stage, I don't want anybody to think we're onto Logan. Portia has extra security around, and sounds like Elyssia will be under her watchful eye. As soon as we have anything concrete, I'll be straight onto her."

I'm happy to step into a warm house after freezing my balls off hanging around alleys and dealing with Mac. I'm honest when I say I don't believe he'll survive long. I bet we're not the only ones who wanted a "friendly chat."

Seth's rooted to his usual spot on the sofa, and I pause when I see a laptop open on his lap. "Don't worry, I'm not allowed the Wi-Fi password." He doesn't turn around, and I continue past him, expecting the others are in the kitchen.

Nobody.

I check Joss's study. Ewan sits at the desk, pouring over a book. "Are you *reading* now?"

He places a finger on the page to mark his place and looks around. "I'm trying to find the creature that attacked Joss. Maybe there's a reference in a book, since I haven't found anything online. Older magic, older enemy?"

"Maybe."

"How did things with Mac go?"

"Great, but not so great. Where's Joss? We can talk about this together."

Ewan laughs softly. "He's outside with Vee."

"Doing what?"

"See for yourself." He gestures towards the back of the house and returns to his book.

Vee's shrieking sets me on high alert, and I rush to the kitchen door with Heath.

I am not prepared for what I witness outside.

Joss and Vee are covered in snow, their jackets and black beanies now white. Vee's hair hangs damp around her red-cheeked face as she laughs and dodges Joss's attempt to tackle her to the ground.

I watch for a few stunned moments as Heath walks into the fray and grabs snow from the ground. A distracted Joss yells at him as Heath deftly shoves the handful down the back of his jacket.

Vee's laughter peels again, and I'm shocked when the sound fills me with a warmth to counteract the cold. When did I last hear Vee laugh with genuine happiness? Have I ever heard this?

Joss now tussles with Heath, and Vee takes advantage of their distraction to land a snowball on Heath's bare head. He releases Joss, and she shrieks and runs as he strides after her.

I cross my arms, debating whether to join in but also knowing I won't have a choice unless I walk back into the house. Grumpy Ewan's already bowed out of the fun.

"Xander! C'mon." A snowball lands squarely in my chest, and my knee-jerk response is to return the attack.

Something overtakes me, and I'm pulled out of a world where demons breathe down my neck and into this snowy white one evolving in front of me. Most years, snow arrives if we're in England during winter, and a snowball fight always ensues.

Talking about Mac can wait. I want some of Vee's positive vibes, to forget and do something I rarely do— unwind and have fun.

$\mathcal{V}$EE

$\mathcal{I}$ tussle with Heath, gasping out protests as he rewards my attack with his own. Cold water trickles down my neck as the snow he pushed into my jacket melts and I tear myself from his arms. Backing up, I beckon him to me.

"I can knock you to the ground if you do that again! Joss already discovered. Ask him."

"War, Vee?" Heath laughs and bends down to scoop more snow. "I don't need to tackle you to hit you with snow."

I side step his missile and poke my tongue out at him before grabbing my own handful. Glancing back at Joss, I halt in surprise.

Xander. Fighting Joss, throwing snowballs as if playing a tennis game.

Laughing.

Bloody hell.

I flinch as a snowball hits me in the back and spin around. "You're mean, Heath. You're going to regret this."

Before he has a chance to respond, I launch myself at him, and my strength knocks him backwards until he sprawls onto his arse. He laughs up at me and holds a hand out, supposedly for help pulling him to his feet.

I cross my arms. "I'm not that stupid!"

"Help Joss with Xander." He points at where Xander skilfully dodges Joss's snowballs, easily hitting him. Snow hangs from Joss's jacket and sleeves. "I want to see what happens if Xander loses."

The childish glee takes over as I stockpile snowballs in front of myself, keeping an eye on the distracted pair. Heath appears at my side and grabs my face in his freezing cold hands before planting a cold mouth on mine. I shy away from his touch, tensing in case I feel snow down my neck next.

"Don't you dare," I warn as he releases me and takes one of my snowballs.

"Not for you." Heath winks as he lobs the snow across

the space between us and smacks his brother in the shoulder. "These are for him."

I almost feel sorry for Xander as all three of us pelt him with snow, especially as his reaction is retaliation with a smile rather than storming back into the house. He can dodge some of our barrage, but not all.

Then he does something that shocks me. Xander straightens, lifts his arms upwards, and palms out in a gesture of surrender. The snow in my hand sticks to my glove instead of heading in his direction as he walks toward me. Eyes trained on mine, we meet in our usual challenge, silently weighing each other up. Like Heath, Xander has no gloves on, and his ice-cold fingers curl around my wrist.

"Are you surrendering, Xander?" I whisper. My breath mists around my face and mingles with the same around him.

"I never surrender to you." His mouth tips upwards at one corner

"Yes, you do."

My heart rate picks up further as he moves his face closer. "Not this time."

Before I can catch up to what he's doing, he seizes the snow from my hand and smears it into my hair.

"Omigod!" I shove at him with the force that would destabilise the others but barely touches him.

Xander laughs and picks at the snow in my hair, while I pout. "You're going to regret that, Pony Boy."

The ground moves as somebody takes hold of me, and I find myself slung over Joss's shoulder, my hair hanging downwards. He has a strong hold around my waist and I grip his jacket as he charges away from Xander.

"Joss! Put me down."

"Huh, I'm rescuing you from Xander."

"I do not need rescuing," I retort and wriggle against him.

I'm dizzy as Joss swings in another direction and calls Ewan's name. I move my head and see Ewan standing in the doorway, holding a beer, and sharing the others' amusement.

"You're playing with fire there," he calls. "Don't upset Vee or she'll bury you in the snow."

"Listen to him," I reply and attempt to loosen Joss's fingers.

"Do you want to land on your head?" he asks.

"Do you want to be in trouble with me?"

"Yes, please." Joss laughs and smacks my backside. "I'll look forward to it."

He sets me upright again, and I stagger, woozy from the blood running from my head. Joss's mouth twitches into a smile, and he leans forward to whisper, "You won't win against me either."

I wrap my arms around his neck. "We'll see about that." My lips touch his as I speak, and I step back with a smirk. "Are you coming outside, Ewan?" I ask.

"Looks like you four are ready for a break." He lifts up his bottle. "Maybe later."

"Boring sod," calls out Heath and rewards Ewan with a snowball to the chest. "Can't have you missing out."

Ewan gives him the middle finger and turns back into the house. "Don't stress, he normally needs a few more beers before he's any fun. You'd think Xander would be the fun police, but nope."

I screw my face up. "He's right though, I'm getting cold now."

Joss's face switches to concern. "Sorry."

"Don't be, I got you all too."

Leaving behind the others and their snowy fun, I walk after Ewan and catch up to him in the kitchen, where he's setting beers on the table next to a pack of playing cards. We've not spoken much recently, and I always feel the tension when we're alone. He shakes his fringe from his face and for the first time in a while smiles at me.

"You're a mess, Vee."

I shiver despite the warmth I stepped into. "Why didn't you join us?"

"I was about to, but think I was too late." He approaches and pulls my damp glove off, before surrounding my icy fingers with his warm ones. "Bloody hell, you *are* cold."

I almost joke to Ewan that he could warm me up, but I sense his wariness and decide not to make things awkward. "I'm okay, I'm about to change."

"It's good to see you relaxed." Ewan pushes a strand of damp hair from face. "I'm happy to see you smile."

"Why didn't you join in?"

He wrinkles his nose. "I don't like the snow. Pisses me off because I can't ride my bike if the roads freeze over. I kinda need that escape right now."

Ewan's look grows wary. Is this a Ewan-style attempt to open up about the other night?

"I think it's important to have your own space."

He pulls off my other glove and watches as he rubs my red hand. "I'm sorry I pushed you away, Vee. I shouldn't have said those things to you."

"No, I needed to hear them." I dip my head. "Look at me, Ewan."

His grip tightens as his eyes meet mine. "Joss said you've changed your mind."

"You opened my eyes to what I was asking, Ewan. I wouldn't only destroy myself in the process, I'd destroy us too." My heart hurts again, as he falls silent and I ache for him to understand and believe my words.

"I'm glad." My pulse kicks up a notch as I look back into his green eyes, sensing the barrier still there.

Pulling my hands from his, I place them both on his cheeks. "I want to get close to you, Ewan. Please don't hold back from me."

He smiles and wipes a hand along my cool cheek, before tipping my face upwards. "I doubt I'd be able to, even if I tried."

His words surge a happiness through me to match how I felt outside, and I break into a smile as he searches my face with his fingers. "You really are bloody cold though. You're shivering, and I'm sure that's not just because of me."

I poke my tongue out at his joke.

"We'll talk later." He kisses my lips briefly. "We'll figure this out. Go change."

"Sorry you can't ride your bike," I say with a smile. "I'd like to join you sometime."

He chuckles. "You hated my bike."

"I just need more practice."

"Okay, some time when it's safer." He points at the table. "Downtime, a few drinks, and maybe wiping the floor with Xander at poker might help."

"I don't play poker."

"I'll teach you, but I'm not playing with Seth." He picks up the cards and taps the box against his chin. "Seth's poker face is too good."

I hang my fluffy white towel on the door and look between the bath and shower as I peel off my damp top. The large tub looks more inviting; I deserve a soak in the bath today, if we're pausing in our crazy crusade for a few hours. I begin to fill the bath and soon water steams into the room, joined by the aroma from the vanilla bath gel I locate in the cupboard. I pull off the rest of my wet clothes and dump them on the floor.

As I swish the water, I decide if this is 'me' time while the guys play poker, I'll need a book to read too. Grabbing a towel from the chair in the corner, I wrap it around myself and head back to Joss's room. He has a few stacked on his dresser, but I'll avoid the ones he uses for research. I don't want supernatural stories joining my peaceful bath.

As I pass the top of the stairs, Seth appears and halts eyes widening. I grip the towel knot at my chest, aware it doesn't go past my knees. Fleetingly, I wonder how often Seth sees girls naked—or semi-naked—as he looks at a point behind my head instead, cheeks pink.

"Sorry, Vee."

"No, you're okay, I'm the one wandering round half-naked. I didn't think." Often I'll walk between the bathroom and a bedroom in just my underwear, never uncomfortable around the men I live with. I thank the stars I chose a towel today and avoided embarrassment.

"I was going to take a shower while you were all busy. I didn't want to get in the way. I thought you were just changing." He stammers out an excuse, and continues to look past me.

"All good. I can take a bath later if you want to use the shower?"

"It's fine. I'll come back." Seth finally looks at me and

fails to stop himself flicking a gaze the length of me; at least his look doesn't linger anywhere but my face.

"Well. Yeah." He turns away to walk back down the stairs and my heart goes out to the lonely guy, excluded by the guys again.

"Seth. If you could be more open with the others about yourself, I think it would help."

He looks back over his shoulder. "There's not much to know I haven't shared. Surely they don't want to hear my childhood stories, and I can't see them wanting to take part in a bonding session."

I laugh, despite the sadness in his voice. "No. You're probably right."

"I know I keep saying this, but be careful of them, Vee."

"I don't need to be." I tug my towel tighter. "I'm fine, honestly."

"I know they don't tell me everything, so I don't have all the facts. But what I do see is they're struggling. I don't think this chaos we're all fighting will end anytime soon." He pulls off his glasses and examines the lenses, before replacing them and looking back at me. "I think it's here to stay."

15

Vee

I'm unsure how many strings Portia needed to pull to allow all six of us to the fundraising weekend at Alasdair's Scottish country estate. Ewan explained the Horsemen's finances allow them to buy into situations. If there's one thing a charity likes, it's promises of large sums of money, so that helped Portia persuade the Foundation to allow six delegates. Joss jokes that siphoning corrupt organisations' bank accounts is starving them, so his powers are being used in the right way.

So, six places are "bought." Three delegates and three partners. The guys calmed down about the affront to their sexuality, but Seth couldn't hide his amusement at the long and complicated discussion over who would 'be' with who. Due to his need to police Seth almost at all times, Xander and Seth are paired up. Who knows how that'll work out? Not well. Joss has his wish and Heath is his partner.

Leaving me with Ewan.

Is this deliberate? A ploy by the others to matchmake us like we're Giant Pandas or another endangered species who need to get it on? Since our talk, Ewan has lost his wariness around me, and although we're more relaxed around each other's company, his affection remains at touches or hugs.

I made a mistake suggesting I could lose my humanity. Each passing day, the Vee who loves the guys pushes away the strange voice that intrudes sometimes and I vow to fight this.

Heath and Xander's news about Logan shocked us, but Logan's demon connection calms my fears about the darkness inside. It's obvious his actions were an attempt to cause division between us and the fae, and perhaps each other too. But we all know the darkness exists; all Logan did was point out and trigger the hidden fears.

There was a short debate over whether we should tell Portia straightaway but reached the consensus that we find concrete proof, and not just the words of a lowlife dealer. As Xander says, she's protected, more so since the attack, and after our investigations here, we'll switch to following him up.

The drive to the estate takes six hours, and we travel in every car, Ewan on his bike. I think all four vehicles is overkill, and Heath whispers to me that Xander wants to show off his car amongst the other prestige vehicles. Xander informed me it's because he wants anybody suspicious to know he's there. Personally, I think the six of us will be a big indicator to anybody demonic or otherwise that we mean business. And not the kind of business most attendees mean. There's debate whether we should stop half way for a night, but Xander rightly—although brusquely—informs us that this isn't a UK touring holiday.

I chose to travel with Heath and Seth in his car. A winter trip on Ewan's bike doesn't appeal, and Heath's has the most room. I nod off somewhere between Yorkshire and the Scottish border, waking to the West Highland's rugged landscape. Snow covers the surrounding countryside and when we leave the motorway for smaller roads, the snow reaches the edge. I'm grateful no more falls while we drive; I don't want to face snowdrifts or accidents.

We arrive at the estate late afternoon, driving through the tall trees along the narrow road leading further away from local villages we passed through. As we approach, a helicopter flies overhead, and I watch open mouthed as it descends towards the opposite side of the property.

Portia wasn't joking about the money involved here.

Cars sporting personal number plates fill a parking area, the prestige models vying for top spot. An Audi TT catches my eye. Red. Convertible—not that anybody would use that in a Scottish winter. I daydream for a moment, picturing myself driving the car and smile at myself. I'm a Horseman, so why hasn't anybody offered me my steed yet?

I climb out of the car into the frosty afternoon. Grey clouds heavy with more snow give the day a strange light. Evening arrives early in this part of the country, and the peaks surrounding us like sentinels already fade into the gloom.

The magnificent property mixes old grey stone with a modern atrium built to enjoy the views. Two storeys high and several times bigger than the guys' place, the building even sports a small turret.

"Do you think the vampires live up there?" pipes up Seth and points. He's shot a look from Ewan and Xander, and he rolls his eyes. "Sense of humour lacking again?"

In addition to the sudden cold from stepping out with

no jacket comes an immediate discomfort as we approach the people grouped close to the house front. A young woman dressed in a smart skirt suit, long brown hair touching her shoulder, stands, tablet and stylus in her hands, as she addresses the delegates in front of her. We wait behind the two men in business suits with their wheeled suitcases.

She indicates which direction they should walk, and they wander away, talking loudly as the girl turns her attention to us.

Seth stays close to my right-hand side, the guys on my left. The relationship between the five of them remains shaky, but Seth's decision to stay quiet and not interfere helps, especially with Xander. I've sensed his disagreement several times, but Seth backs down as soon as Xander's temper rises along with his voice.

The girl looks up, and I wait for the inevitable reaction. None. She's in a hurry, flustered as she glances behind us at others approaching. The woman runs a finger along the screen. "Six? You must be the Alexander Landon group?"

I snap my head around. I was completely unaware Xander wasn't his full name.

"Correct," he replies.

"Okay. Three rooms." She sweeps a calculating look between the six of us. "You're in the coach house." The girl points in the direction of a small, single storey building separate to the main, but built with the same materials, surrounded by trees and lawn.

"Most of the larger groups are staying in the new conversions, such as the gate house and old stables. You can take a look at where your money will be spent as some of the rehab patients will be living there."

The woman drops a set of keys into Xander's hand, one

set into Heath's, and one into Seth's. She looks between me and Seth with a smile. "Your room is the one at the end of the hallway. The welcome session starts in half an hour."

Our party strides along the stone path that leads from the main house to the coach house, the guys with their rucksacks and me wheeling a suitcase. This is the most bizarre weekend break I've ever taken.

Xander strides ahead with Joss and Ewan, and Heath hangs back with me and Seth. "Interesting that out of all of us, the girl thought you're with Seth."

I glance at Seth. "Why's that odd?"

"Do I really have to tell you? Look at him, then look at us."

I nudge him. "Such modesty. How about I go back and inform the woman he's the only one I'm *not* in a relationship with?"

Heath fixes his gaze on Seth. "As long as he doesn't think if he's in our group he can join us."

Seth grips his rucksack. "Sorry, Heath, you're not my type."

Heath's stunned look amuses me, and we watch as Seth hurries to keep up with the other three. I poke Heath. "Don't be rude to Seth. He already feels on the edge. If you upset him, he might leave."

"I doubt he will. Not now he knows what's really out there waiting for him."

A small courtyard leads to a red-painted front door and Xander leads the way inside. The words "rustic charm" come to mind as we step into a wood-panelled hallway and tiled floor.

Xander stands in one of the room's doorways, arms crossed, rucksack at his feet, with a deep frown on his face. Two other doors are open too.

"What's wrong?" asks Heath as he approaches.

"They're all fucking double beds."

Besides me, Seth chews the side of his hand. "I'll sleep on the floor."

"Correct," replies Xander. "If you're sharing with me."

"We already decided who was sharing with who," says Joss.

"How do you normally choose who Vee sleeps with?" Seth asks. "Or do you all share the same bed?"

Seth's question drops a heavy silence from a great height and knocks the conversation dead. "That's not really your business is it?" replies Ewan in a low voice.

"I'm just curious," he says and walks to an open door. "I'll leave my things in here."

What shocks me the most in this situation is that several weeks ago the suggestion I'd share a bed with two guys would fill me with horror. Now, it feels like it would be like sharing with family. Portia's comments about being between the brothers heated my cheeks, but in a way there'd be something different than the innuendo she filled the question with. They care. Despite the strange bond, the human emotions I fooled myself I could lose exist between us all. The guys love and would do anything to keep each other safe, and I'm now included in that.

I rub a finger across my lips as I look at the back of Xander's head. Even he showed me how he feels through his kiss the other day.

I remember the image in the book Joss showed me and again reject the idea. Apart from the logistics, the idea of time between squabbling siblings doesn't conjure up particularly sexy images.

"Vee?" asks Joss. "What are you smirking about?"

"Nothing." The smirk remains as I walk into the room. A

window opposite looks across a nearby field and towards the Highland backdrop, a scene that trumps the countryside around Oxfordshire.

The beams in the low ceiling are painted white to match the walls and I'm relieved to see a radiator below the window, warming the room. I sit on the edge of the wrought iron bed. Isn't this a bit overkill for a rehab facility?

"I'll have this room, I like the view." I turn to the doorway.

Only Ewan and Xander remain.

Xander rubs his face. "Don't hang around, I want to get up to the main building as soon as possible and take a look."

I sigh. Back to operating at lightning speed.

16

Vee

Xander doesn't get his wish to snoop around because when we arrive at the main building people are funnelled towards a large room, ready for a talk from the guy we're dying to meet. I've never attended a business conference, and I'm unsure of etiquette. As we enter the old building, we're shown a low table beneath an old coat of arms where lanyards and foundation brochures are placed. The same girl as before stands by the table and hands us small plastic bags as we approach.

Ewan peers inside as we walk towards the room we're shepherded to. "What is this shit?"

"Pens." Joss pulls one out then rummages around inside the bag. "Hey, Xan look."

Xander refused to take his bag, and when Joss throws a soft pink ball at his head, his face sours.

"Stress ball!" laughs Joss. "I think you should have this."

"Grow up," mutters Xander and passes him, leaving the item on the floor.

A young woman nearby laughs and bends to pick it up. "Looks like he might need this."

Her long red hair and freckles match her Scottish accent. "I'm Breanna." She holds a hand out to Joss. "Nice to meet you."

I wait for Joss's charming smile, but when he takes her hand, his eyes widen.

Crap. Demon? We've only been here an hour.

He returns Breanna's greeting, and she nods at the rest of us as she passes by. She stands out and not because of her unusual hair colour, but due to the casual jeans and heavy blue jumper amongst the business-attired delegates.

"Joss?" asks Heath.

"I think she's a demon. In fact I'm pretty sure she is, but I also think I know her." Confusion lines Joss's face as he stares after the woman.

"As long as she isn't a past hook-up," replies Heath.

"Didn't you hear me?" he snaps. "Demon?"

"Whoa. Touchy."

Joss chews on his lips as he watches her go. "She probably just has one of those faces."

"What faces?" asks Ewan.

"Just... familiar." Joss shakes himself out of his thoughts.

"Odd you'd come across a demon a second time," Seth puts in. "I thought you killed them?"

A passing man, dressed in slacks and a shirt with a yellow jumper draped over his shoulder, double takes at Seth's words.

"Shut up," growls Ewan.

Xander strides off. "Yeah, come on."

I exchange a look with Joss. I detected something too,

but not as strongly. Breanna would be aware that shaking hands with Joss means he'd be aware what she is. Why not disguise herself?

In the large room, we sit on a row of upholstered chairs and wait for Alasdair to take his place at the lectern set up at the front. This isn't what I expected, but what did I expect? Seth spends time rooting through his bag and examining the contents. I'm becoming used to his avoidance tactics, but also I wish he'd try to involve himself more. I know the guys are intimidating, but they need to forge more trust.

When Xander announced he'd share a room with Seth, I didn't miss Seth's horrified look. The reason why is obvious —Xander's obsessed with the guy and convinced he'll run. Does he still think Seth's involved in Casey's disappearance?

A man appears and stands at the lectern. He's middle-aged, hair peppered with grey, and his eyes a slate-blue colour to match his buttoned shirt. He holds the demeanour of someone who's used to attention, and his immaculate clothes would give Seth a run for his money.

The buzz of conversation stops as he greets everybody in a faded Scottish accent. "Good afternoon, and I'd like to welcome you all to my humble home and thank you for joining me. I hope you'll learn enough about my projects to turn your generous donations into regular contributions."

He projects a warm and friendly smile across the room and elicits some laughter.

"Let me explain a little more about my recent project and plans for the estate. Some of you have already found the new accommodation, which I hope you'll find very comfortable. Some of the staff who'll be working with the clients will take you for a short tour of the new facilities tomorrow and explain our program. We don't have any clients here yet, but I know there are representatives from hospitals and community services here. I hope you all find time to talk. We have some functions arranged, starting with tonight's meet and greet, and I hope to chat with some of you there."

The guys remain silent throughout the remainder of his speech, and I listen carefully. My lie detecting skills will be questioned by the four, especially since we already spotted one demon, and I pick up nothing but the truth. Seth makes notes on the back of the brochure we were given, whereas Heath leans forward elbows on knees, and hands beneath his chin listening as intently as me.

I sense Joss's continuing unease, as he holds the stress ball between his hands and digs his nails in. He scans the room after we sit, his gaze landing on the demon girl perched on a seat at the end in the front row.

Alasdair finishes his power point presentation with an announcement about tonight's cocktail party and another hope we'll all be able to network with each other. Some stop and chat outside as we leave the room, business professionals who could mutually benefit from networking.

Then there's us.

I hope nobody asks me what my job is; if they do, I'll ask my "partner" to explain.

Ewan stands, arms crossed as he watches the delegates pass from the room. He's attempted "casual business" clothing but can't pull the look off in the same way the others manage. Maybe it's his refusal to tame his unruly hair, or the tattoos poking out from under his black shirt. Mostly, it's his attitude—the guy looks like he wants to run rather than network.

The urge to kiss him, to take his hand and tell him not to stress pushes through, but I stop myself. We need another conversation, but each time I try, he changes the subject.

Now we're sharing a room for two nights, the conversation won't be avoided much longer.

Behind me, Xander leans in to read the notice pinned to a tall metal stand, beside the black-clothed table containing the bags and business cards.

"The businesses attending are listed. Nova Pharm is one of them and a few others I recognise."

"Anybody's names?" asks Heath.

"No."

"Looks like we'll be attending the cocktail party," I reply. "Will you recognise anybody if they are connected to the Order or the fae?"

Xander steps back. "Some. Mostly we know names, not faces. If Breanna is a demon, I'm sure we'll soon find more."

Ewan holds up his lanyard hung by a blue cord with the company name printed. "We can look at their names. I still have the lists on my laptop."

"Lots of mingling then." Ewan pulls a face at Joss's words.

A group pass by, chatting and oblivious as they walk along the maroon-carpeted hallway towards stairs with a wrought iron bannister, sweeping up into another part of the house.

"I'm not ending this evening without taking a bloody good look round this place," Xander says in a low voice. "That Alasdair guy has something to hide, however friendly and human he is."

"What are you expecting to find?" asks Seth.

"Answers," retorts Xander.

Delegate staff, wearing different coloured lanyards, mingle with the attendees stationed by the stairs and hallways. They're not security, but there's an air that they're keeping people out of other parts of the house. Understandable, there must be a lot of valuable items in here, but I share Xander's curiosity and hope more answers lie within these walls.

"I'm headed back to the room to change," says Ewan, pulling at his shirt collar.

"I don't think jeans and Converse are included in tonight's dress code," Joss replies. "Sorry, mate."

"For fuck's sake. Well, I'm going back to rest then."

"No idea why you insisted on riding your bike up here in this weather," says Heath. "Crazy."

Ignoring Heath, Ewan heads away, as if remaining in the building a moment longer might suffocate him as much as his shirt collar.

17

*J*OSS

I straighten my sleeves as I look back at my reflection.

Something isn't right.

I sense it, but there's nothing concrete.

I don't voice this to the guys, but Vee's picked up my uncertainty.

The red-haired woman, Breanna, I'm know she's a demon, and she also lives somewhere in my brain's dark recesses, but where? We've come across many people over the years; of course I won't be able to remember every face, but I *know* her.

I study my face more closely. I don't look any different; I'm fully recovered inside and out, but the unease is back. Not the unsettling sensations from the parasitic demon, but a deeper one in the pit of my stomach. The guy looking back at me is Joss Smith, whoever he is. Of course we've researched our names to find any connection to real people —alive or dead—and found nothing. So Joss is me. Isn't he? My head and stomach lurch as I hear the man's voice and the sound of a gun firing, the same as in my vision when I died, as real as if he was in the room with me.

The man in the mirror pales and my heart rate speeds as other images from the dream, or whatever the hell it was, attempt to loop in again. I force them away and take a shuddering breath. This keeps happening. I've spoken to Vee and mentioned I had a vision to the guys, but I don't know how to explain to them the full situation. I know I have to, and I will, but the Collector spooked them enough, when he told us he's met Horsemen before. I'll speak to Vee again and then sit down and talk. Maybe after a few beers.

Ready to face the evening, I walk into the hallway between the rooms in the coach house and rap on Vee and Ewan's door.

Vee answers and opens the door wide. "Just in time! Ewan disappeared and I need somebody to zip my dress."

"Yeah, he went with Heath to look around the outside of the estate."

Vee's hair shines, loose around her shoulders, and her subtle make-up accentuates her delicate features, the gloss on her lips shining invitingly.

"You look beautiful." I plant a kiss on her cheek.

Her eyes shine too. "Thank you."

Vee turns and walks into the room. She lifts her long brown hair to expose her neck and the unzipped dress. Vee's delicate floral fragrance fills the room, stronger as I walk closer. As I help, my fingers brush her skin and immediately feel the buzz from her thoughts. I lean forward to place my lips on the back of her neck, and she shivers.

"Thanks." Vee turns and smiles up at me. "Are you feeling better?"

"I'm fine."

Vee places a hand on my cheek, and her lips against mine, the same lips as always but tasting of the pink lipstick she's wearing. "Have you told anybody else how you feel?"

"No. It's okay. I think this is linked to what happened when I was attacked. It's made me jittery."

Her hair shines, and I resist the urge to hold her and bury my face into it. Why am I feeling vulnerable like this?

She smudges the lipstick from my lips with her thumb. "Only a half truth, Joss. You're not okay. What's happening?"

"I'm fine, just hoping you don't make any more of your odd requests to turn you into a monster."

Vee's face darkens. "Don't joke about it, Joss. You know I've backed away from that decision. Why say that now?"

I stroke her hair. "And we're happy you have. *I'm* happy you have. I care about you and don't want to lose you."

"And I think that's why. The love I have for you guys, and yours for me, stops me wanting to take that route."

I smile and stroke her soft cheek with my thumb. "Are you saying you love me?"

Vee's eyes soften, and she nods. "Of course. You all know that."

My whole chest warms at her words, as if she's wrapped herself around my heart. "Good. Because I sure as hell love you, but I think you already knew that."

She stands on tiptoes and kisses me, arms around my neck. "Yes. But, I need to tell you all. Focus on those emotions and build our unity. That's the only way we'll stay strong."

"But you're still fighting something, aren't you?"

She drops her gaze. "Yes. The desire to become powerful

drives me sometimes, and I don't understand why, but how I feel about you all interferes."

"Well, whatever else is happening, I think the Vee in front of me is who you really are." I tip her chin. "I think you fought something and won."

She doesn't respond, sits on the bed, and slips on her shoes. Her dress's skirt rides up her legs, revealing her slim calves, and I'm overwhelmed with the sudden desire to push her back onto the bed and cover her body with mine. Screw the party.

"Where's Seth?" she asks, and I blink away the images.

"With Xander, of course. Lucky guy has a personal bodyguard."

"I don't think Seth sees it that way," she says with a laugh.

"Yeah, he doesn't want to come to this evening, but like the rest of us, he has no choice."

"But I like when my Pony Boys dress up in suits." Vee arches a brow. She stands again, matching my height in her heels, and straightens my tie. "I'll need to keep an eye on you all in case someone tries to steal you away from me."

"Yeah, right. As if that's gonna happen." I slap her backside. "And don't call us that. It reminds me of Portia."

Vee slaps mine in return and wanders over to the nightstand. She places her phone in a small handbag. "I'm surprised Portia didn't want to attend. She loves human attention."

"I suspect the real reason is she's worried fae might be here. The Scottish fae court and hers aren't great friends."

"Aha. How many courts are there in the UK?"

"England, Wales, Scotland, and another in Ireland. As you can imagine the Irish is the strongest and with the most influence."

"Why?"

I smooth her hair. "I need to lend you more lore books, don't I? All the fae mythology began there. Some of it's just fairy stories, of course."

"I see what you did there. Clever." Vee picks up her bag. "I wish the place was totally free from anything supernatural. I'd like a night that doesn't end in death."

"This isn't a weekend break, Vee. You knew that."

"Yes. Maybe ask the demons to wait at least one night before raining chaos on the world." When I don't reply, she walks to the door. "Come on. Let's find your date for tonight. Where did you say Heath was again?"

She laughs, but I can't lighten the situation like she can.

I'd like a night that doesn't end in death, too.

18

V EE

*O*ur group are later than some as we waited for
Heath and Ewan to return from the scouting trip.
Exploring the huge estate took longer than they expected,
and they didn't manage to cover everywhere. They found
nothing; tonight the guys aim to check out the house more
thoroughly. We walk inside to couples milling around in the
large hallway. I'm relieved I chose a dress midway between
casual and formal, although it was bloody freezing walking
across here from the coach house until Heath wrapped his
arms around my naked shoulders.

A group break away from the chatter and walk up the
staircase. Xander gestures, and I hold the black metal
bannister as we follow the group up the winding stairs.
Another sign indicates which way to go, and walk and along
another wood-panelled corridor.

"This place is huge," remarks Joss.

"A lot to check out." Xander pauses and looks at a family portrait hung on the wall. The painting depicts a woman, man, and two boys, and a metal plaque attached to the bottom reads "Faulkner Family 1864."

Seth whispers, "Look out for the moving eyes."

Ewan frowns at him. "What?"

"Scooby Doo? Mysterious paintings with people hidden behind?"

Ewan looks to me. "What is your friend talking about now?"

"A TV show. The Scooby gang hunted monsters. Not quite the same as you guys though." Seth chuckles. "Although you're a bit shaggy, Ewan."

I frown at Seth and shake my head at him. Why does he insist on annoying Ewan?

A woman in a tight, black dress passes and gives us a curious look. Heath and Joss face away from her, and I don't miss her appreciative appraisal as she walks by.

The floorboards creak beneath the thick carpet as we follow the trail of people heading to the evening cocktail session. Inside a large room, food stands and small, white plates line the table beside wine glasses. Ewan strides over and takes hold of a plate, and I join him as he wrinkles his nose at the food in front of him. Small cupcakes iced in a blue to match the company colours are arranged on a stand, and tiny, savoury pastries and sandwiches alongside.

"I'm bloody starving," he mutters. He picks up a mini quiche between forefinger and thumb and examines it. "Is this all we get?"

"Looks like it."

"Bloody hell," he mutters and loads his plate.

Apart from tables, there's no furniture in the room,

forcing attendees to huddle in groups and break out to chat if they feel like doing so.

As I help myself to the strange assortment, a waitress walks by and offers us a drink from wine glasses on a silver tray.

As the hours pass, I'm less comfortable. Joss is still in a weird mood, Ewan and Seth are equally uncomfortable, and Xander's back in alert mode. That doesn't help. Only Heath takes things in his stride, but he worked with me at Alphanet and the human business world isn't as far from his comfort zone. Seth's mood lifted since his world expanded beyond the farmhouse, but I sense he's pleased he's surrounded by the Horsemen, despite his protests. I'm uncomfortable, as if I'm under scrutiny although as usual the guys receive more. Seth breaks away to find something to eat, under Xander's watchful eye.

"Go with him." Heath pokes Xander. "Keep an eye on your *man*."

Joss snorts in amusement and Xander glares. "I don't see you two holding hands."

"Aww!" Joss slings an arm across Heath's shoulders and rests his head against his hair. "He's not into PDAs. No cuddles from Heath."

Heath pushes him away. "Seriously, dude. Too far."

"What? Are you upset about what happened earlier? I swear I wasn't doing anything with Ewan, it was just coincidence we were both naked."

I choke on my wine as Joss's eyes gleam with amusement; I'm happy he's dropped the tension from earlier. This is my Joss, whether he's a front for how he feels is another question.

"I was not naked with Joss!" protests Ewan loudly.

A woman in the group beside us turns her head then quickly looks away again when she meets my eyes.

"Will you stop drawing attention to us," mutters Xander.

Joss smiles and looks into his wine glass as Xander heads after Seth. Heath moves away from Joss, arms crossed and face dark. Before I can say anything too, he straightens. "Well, I'm still bloody hungry. I'm going to see if there's any food left."

We're left in silence, and reality wraps around us again. I grip my glass and close my eyes, attempting to sense more demon presence. I wasn't joking when I told Joss I didn't want tonight to end in death.

There's something ego-boosting about being surrounded by men who other women in the room are drawn to, and having the guys completely oblivious. In the past, even on dates, most men I've known can't help checking out the girls around them. These guys? I'm amused they only check out the women in the room to see if they're demons.

One or two people have approached to chat, but nobody in our group is particularly sociable. I haven't missed some women's unprofessional sizing up of the guys, and I've seen them weighing up which of the five I'm with too.

If only they knew...

A middle-aged, business-suited guy ensures he introduces himself to everybody, and when he approaches for our turn, I glance around the room for Heath. How badly did Joss piss him off? Because he's not by the food. Chewing a nail, I look around the room, but Heath's tall figure isn't amongst any of the groups.

Tiptoeing and sliding my hand up Joss's arm to get his attention I whisper, "I'm going to the bathroom."

"Do you want one of us to come with you?"

"Seriously?" I point to a discreet sign close to the door at the opposite end of the room. "I think I can get there safely."

Joss nods and leans in to brush his lips against mine, our natural goodbye.

"Where are you going?" asks Xander as he notices.

"Bathroom."

"Oh." He blows air into his cheeks. "Don't be long."

Ewan nods. "Yeah. Be careful."

I shake my head with a smile at their protectiveness and make my way out of the room. The hallway matches the one we walked through earlier, wood panelling and portraits; floor creaking beneath the carpet. A few people mill about chatting in pairs, and as I move along the corridor, I catch sight of Heath.

A woman stands opposite him, and I pause to watch them. I know this is a networking weekend, but I can't help the jealousy that rises. She's attractive—and that's just from the back. Long legs and an elegant black dress that gloves her curvy figure, and long glossy brown hair, straightened to perfection.

Heath has his hands in his pockets, and the woman seems to be doing the talking, judging by all her hand gestures and his bored expression. Did she pick Heath out because she thought I was with another of the guys?

I walk over and slide my hand around Heath's taut waist. He left his suit jacket over a chair back with the group, and as I rest my head on his cotton shirt, the scent of his cologne joins the warmth of his body. Turning my face upwards, I meet his relieved eyes, and he kisses me the way Joss did moments ago.

"Verity?"

I jerk my head around in surprise at the familiar voice, and when I meet Charlotte's eyes, I'm unsure who's the most surprised. I'd seen Alphanet listed on the companies attending, but as they're a big organisation, I didn't think twice about who'd be here.

Her plump, pink lips part slightly, and her thoughts couldn't be clearer even if she had them on a flashing neon sign above her head: *you're with him?*

"Hi, Charlotte." I move my arm down, so I'm holding Heath's hand. "How are you? I didn't realise you were here this weekend."

"Same." She stares down at where my fingers lace through Heath's. "Did you move companies? Who are you representing?"

Heath interrupts my pained attempt not to lie. "I was headhunted for a different company. Vee's with me, as my guest."

Charlotte blinks. "That's nice."

Nice. I smile. I can think of better words. The conversation stops before it's even started. For the first time in days, I feel uncomfortably like the awkward human Vee who would fade into the background around girls like Charlotte.

"Everything okay, Vee?" Heath blanks out Charlotte as he turns his attention to me.

"Fine. I just wondered where you'd gone."

"Bathroom. Then I bumped into um..." He pulls an apologetic face. "Sorry, Charlotte, isn't it?"

I fight smiling at his words; he knows Charlotte's name since I used it a minute ago. Her mouth tightens.

"Maybe I'll see you around?" she says to me. "I'd love to catch up and chat about what you've been up to."

"Sure! We're part of a group you'd probably like to meet," interrupts Heath. "What do you think, Vee? You could introduce Charlotte to all your men." His eyes sparkle in amusement as I frown at him. "Did you know Vee has a collection of guys now?"

"Heath, shush." I tighten my fingers around his in warning.

"I like to think I'm her favourite though." He pokes my nose affectionately.

Charlotte's confused look grows.

I force a laugh and dig my nails into Heath's hand. "Yes, because you're so funny."

Heath grins. "Maybe catch you later, Charlotte. I just wanted to chat to Vee about something."

"Oh. Okay." She snaps herself out of her staring between us. "Nice to see you again, and I'll be sure to check out Vee's men collection." Charlotte laughs then stops abruptly when we look back with straight faces.

As she stalks away, I turn to Heath, who wraps his arms around my waist and smiles down at me. "Sorry. I couldn't resist. When I worked at Alphanet, I'd watch Charlotte and her friend, and their superior attitudes to every girl around them annoyed me."

"You didn't have to make a comment about me having a collection of men."

Heath's mouth tips at one corner. "But you do! Besides, I wanted to see her reaction."

I poke his nose the way he did mine. "And don't get any ideas about being my favourite, mister."

Heath places a hand on his heart. "Ouch."

I bite my lip. Is he serious? "Don't be mad. Nobody is my favourite."

"Yeah, I know." His hands roam around to my backside. "But you like me better than Xander, right?"

"Depends on what mood you're both in." I push his hand away.

"Or what mood you're in." He points at his cheek. "Please, will you admit you punched him when you were in a War mood?"

I shake my head. "Will you ever drop that?"

"I wish I'd seen his reaction."

"Heath..."

"Sorry."

"Let's get back to the others. Come on."

Heath pouts at me. "We haven't had much chance to spend time alone together recently."

"Occupational hazard." I kiss him, leaving my mouth pressed on his long enough to feel the soft buzz of connection.

Heath sighs and pushes his hands into the back of my hair before softly kissing me back. "Yeah. Doesn't leave much time for romantic dates, huh?"

"Exactly. I'd suggest a walk around the estate grounds in the snow tomorrow, but you'd probably just shove snow down my jacket."

Heath chuckles and rubs both thumbs across my cheeks. "I'll settle for a kiss."

The second his mouth meets mine; he ignites the spark that's been lost in the middle of recent events. I press mine back, and I'm unprepared for the intensity that follows the softness. Heath kisses me, hungry and needy, and I part my lips as he holds my head to him. He crushes me against him, his strong arm around my waist. His taste, the way his tongue pushes hot into my mouth, the overwhelming need radiating from him, pushes everything away.

Here, now, in this snatched moment, I'm lost in Heath who's skilful kiss draws me into him, and my body floods with a longing I struggle to push away.

"This isn't very professional," I whisper as someone passes by.

Heath nips my earlobe. "If I were totally unprofessional, I'd find a room to hide in with you. Do you want me to tell you what I'd do?"

I shiver at his bite. "Probably not a good idea. I might take you up on anything you suggest."

"I know." He steps back, eyes glinting, and appraises me. "Hell, look at you. You're freaking gorgeous."

I rub lipstick from his mouth with my thumb. "Thank you. You don't look so bad yourself."

"Hmm." Heath pulls at his shirt collar. "I'd rather not be wearing this."

I arch a brow. "You mean you'd rather be naked with me?"

"No. I promised myself we'd spend some time together with our clothes on before we took them off again."

"Fair enough. Maybe we'll take that walk around the estate tomorrow then?"

"I was thinking something less work related." Heath smiles. "Joss took you on a date; I'm sure I can find time too."

I chew my lip at Joss's name. "Can you talk to Joss, please?"

"What? Why?" Heath straightens. "Is he hiding something about how he feels again? What's happening?"

I place a hand on his arm to quell his panic. "Joss is fine. Mostly. He told me about a vision he had, but doesn't want to talk to you guys about it."

"Why not?"

"You know Joss; he'd rather keep things light." I pause. "I

know you have visions too, but Joss said his was clearer this time."

Heath drags a hand through his hair and closes his eyes. "Yeah, we don't talk about those. It's an unspoken agreement between us all because it fucks with our heads. I prefer to ignore them."

"Sorry. I shouldn't have mentioned this, but I don't want another situation where you hide things from each other."

"It's all good. If the vision reached a stage where it bothers Joss, I need to talk to him."

His anxiety reaches me, and I pull Heath's head towards me and kiss him again. Heath's kiss is less insistent and gentler, and I hug him to me. I hope I did the right thing by sharing Joss's problems.

We head back to the main room and are met with concerned looks and words by the others. Joss slides an arm around my waist and kisses my hair, always the most tactile of the four he often does this without thinking. I glance around the room. Charlotte stands a few feet away, and I catch her eye before she quickly looks away.

The temptation to kiss one of the others edges in, but I resist. I can't help the little jolt of smugness at Charlotte's poor attempt to hide her shocked expression.

19

*X*ANDER

I straighten my shirtsleeves and scan the room, taking another good look for Alasdair. Vee's in the centre of our group, relaxed and smiling as she jokes with the other guys. People's reaction amused me when we walked in earlier, Vee holding Joss's hand and Heath's arm around her shoulder. There are dozens of people in the room, and their arrival shut down much of the conversation happening around us. Because of the guys? Or the girl clearly indicating "back off, they're mine"?

Vee keeps asking Seth if he's okay, and her concern for him annoys me still. I share Ewan's opinion he's not one hundred percent what he says, but I'm biding my time. I watch Seth's every move, have done since he joined us, despite Vee chastising me to give the guy some breathing space. I sense genuine discomfort from him at being in tonight's social situation, and he seems physically weak, but what's happening behind the facade? The longer he's with us, the more my suspicion grows.

A girl dressed in a white shirt and black skirt approaches and offers us drinks from a tray. I swig mine and look around for a table to place the empty glass on. There's a guy opposite with a beer. Where do I get one instead of this mouthful?

"I don't normally come to this kind of thing," says Seth in a low voice. "I'm not big on social events."

"I can tell. Just have a few drinks, you'll relax," I say. "I'll keep an eye on you."

Seth snorts. "Yeah, I'm sure you will."

The number of people here makes it difficult to study them all without wandering the room and staring at them all like a lunatic. At least two of us need to get out of the room and explore the place; if demons are here I want to know how many and why. This isn't a big surprise, nor is the fact we've been lured here for a reason. Yeah, well, they'll be sorry when the five of us start on them.

Alasdair hasn't shown his face again, and more than ever, we need him to answer questions. More than that, we need Joss or Vee close enough to him to be able to detect if he's a demon too. The red-haired girl exuded the demonic presence, and she's connected to somebody.

Someone in this room?

Breanna's here now, dressed in a tight-fitting green dress, distinctive red hair spilling down her back. She works the room, chatting to group after group, adding in smiles and touches. The sight sickens me, as if she's taunting us that she can get this close to humans. What worries me more is Breanna's with a human guy, young and attractive, and stuck to her like a guard dog. I'm holding onto the thought demons are unlikely to kill anybody while we're here and draw attention to the place, but what else are demons doing here? If they're not killing, are they looking for new people to possess?

I lower my voice and tell Heath, "I'm gonna find Breanna and talk to her."

He nods and continues his conversation with Joss and Vee.

I walk across the room in another attempt to corner her, but Breanna steps to one side and into a new conversation.

I halt next to a group, and after ten minutes forced to chat about their boring lives, I catch sight of Heath staring at me from across the room. I frown as he holds his hands at waist height and subtly points to the right, and the doorway. Turning my head, a surge of adrenaline joins my surprise.

Logan.

He's with his wife again, immediately and enthusiastically greeted by a younger couple who evidently know him. If we stand out, Logan eclipses us in his tailored suit. He's taller than the average human, and the fae has made no attempt to disguise his unusual appearance. Gazes are drawn to the unusual man with bronze eyes and pale blond hair. I make a hasty excuse to the man droning on about hedge funds—which I've finally figured out isn't a business related to gardening—and weave through the people back to the guys and Vee.

"What the fuck?" I whisper.

"This is good," replies Ewan. "This proves there's a link between them all. He obviously knows people here."

"And Alasdair," puts in Heath. "He must too."

"Has Alasdair arrived yet?" I crane my head, watching Logan approach the red-haired demon as I scan the room. "Whoa. Okay. Could he be any more public?"

The familiarity between the two is confirmed when

Breanna greets him with a warm smile, and he kisses her on the cheek.

"Why behave like that when they know we're here?" I ask. "Right in front of us all."

"Because they want you to see, of course." Seth steps from where he's hidden himself in the corner of us and pushes his glasses against his face. "Who is this man you're all staring at? The fae I've heard you talking about recently?"

We haven't spoken about Logan, or what happened with Mac, in detail, but he's heard the name. I suspect Vee has shared who Logan is, because she looks at the floor rather than at me. I can't blame her. Seth is smart at extracting information.

I nod. "Yeah. Logan. Portia's adviser."

"But you said the girl was a demon. You told me fae don't like demons." A woman a few feet away throws Seth a curious look, and I make a hand gesture to indicate he should keep his voice down.

"Correct. Joss? Vee? Any others here?"

Joss shakes his head. "Honestly, I can't feel any more demons around."

"What the hell is this Alasdair guy doing? Do you think he knows he's working with demons?"

"Oh yeah. Us humans? We're really good at picking up on supernatural creatures we don't believe exist." Seth snorts. "Or maybe he knows, and he's sold them his soul or whatever. Could be how he's so wealthy and good-looking."

"People don't sell their souls to demons," sneers Ewan. "Don't believe what you learn from TV shows and movies."

"Some people will do whatever it takes to get what they want."

"Drop the cryptic shit, Seth," he snaps back. "I'm not in the mood."

"Just saying. Sometimes people are made an offer they can't refuse."

Ewan tips his head and looks at me. When Seth breaks long silences with statements like this, he doesn't help with our trust issues.

"Really? Did someone make *you* an offer you can't refuse?" Ewan asks him.

All eyes turn to Seth who taps the edge of his wine glass and stares at the floor. "No."

I exchange another glance with Ewan. *Lying bastard.* I look to Vee for confirmation, but she shakes her head and mouths "truth" at me.

Shit.

"Forget this distraction." I jerk my head in Logan's direction. "We need to get him somewhere for a cosy chat."

Seth drains his glass, before grabbing another from a passing tray held by the waitress.

"Did Logan see you?" Vee asks.

"I don't know, but he'll expect us to be here. Heath. Come with me."

We leave the other four and walk back to the table laid with food, then take plates and watch Logan from our vantage point. He doesn't move from talking to Breanna, although his wife has moved on to flirt with a younger guy nearby.

I believed Mac, but now I have confirmation. Logan is working against Portia with the Order. Demons and fae are involved with whatever the hell is happening with this charity and are linked to Nova Pharm. Why? And why the fuck are they killing humans and flaunting their alliance in front of us?

Things are adding up, but I can't figure out the whole

equation. I will by the end of tonight because this guy isn't leaving my sight.

"What's the plan?" Heath asks.

"We let Logan know we're here—when he leaves, we follow him. I'm damn sure he'll lead us into something else they've planned for us."

"Then that needs all five of us."

"No. We'll follow Logan, see where he goes, then head back for the others. I think it's better some of us stay here to watch what's happening in the room. Again, in case the idea is to get us all away from here."

"Or they might want to split us up?"

I drag a hand through my hair. "Yeah. Could be either, but this is how I want to handle it."

Heath looks as if he'll protest, but then sighs. "I'll tell the others."

As he walks away, I lick crumbs from my fingers, fired up and ready for this. Finally, Logan turns his head and meets my eyes. We hold each other's gaze, unblinking and silent, and the world falls away. But this isn't star-crossed lovers whose eyes meet across a crowded room, this is a mutual understanding.

Shit is about to change.

20

*V*EE

The evening begins with the room filled by soft, polite conversation and English reservation, but as the time passes, the volume grows and laughter becomes more raucous. I switch from wine to orange juice. It's harder to avoid telling the truth with too much alcohol in my system.

Logan's arrival shocked the guys and me. My mind flooded with the feelings Logan gave me the last time I saw him, but I managed to push down the doubt and fear. He's linked to demons. Of course he was lying that night. Xander spent the best part of the evening stalking him; the people in the room are the jungle he has to work through—or the prey for Logan and the demons. We don't know which yet.

After an hour, Xander and Logan's stand-off ended as Logan left the room, without his wife, and with Breanna. How could Logan and his wife be close to Portia and not arouse suspicion? Unsurprisingly, Xander and Heath followed minutes later. We're all aware that any of these actions could be a ploy, but Death and War are the best to step after them. Despite their sibling issues, they're the most in sync and strongest.

We'll have plenty of chances to dig around if we're here all weekend, but I think that's the issue. Xander wants evidence now, and to leave as soon as possible. I'm surprised Alasdair hasn't made an appearance yet; he struck me as a guy who'd enjoy being the life and soul of an expensive party he organised.

Ewan and Joss have positioned themselves in a better vantage point, and I'm left with Seth.

Seth barely says two words to anybody after his strange words to Ewan, and his face flushes as he drinks enough wine for both of us. His silence is joined by perspiration crossing his brow, and he sways before finally slumping onto a nearby seat.

"Seth, you need fresh air."

He looks back at me, his pale blue eyes awash with the wine he's drunk.

"I don't usually drink much, Vee. I think I had too much."

"Uh huh." I help him to his feet. "Let's take a walk into that bracing November weather. That'll slap some sobriety into you."

He smiles back at me. "Yeah. What about the guys? Won't they be worried?"

"What about?"

"You and me disappearing. You should tell one of them."

"Oh. Hang on."

I walk over to Ewan, whose boredom level matches Joss beside him. "Guys, I'm taking Seth out for some air." Ewan opens his mouth. "Don't follow me. You're supposed to be keeping an eye on things while Xander and Heath aren't around."

Ewan straightens and cranes his head to look at Seth, now leaning forward with his head in his hands. "Doom*Geek* can't hold his drink, huh?"

"I don't blame him for trying to blank his mind for a few hours," I say. "I'll take him outside before he pukes on the floor."

"Don't be long," Ewan warns. "I don t like the idea of you alone with him."

"I think we all know I can defend myself. He also knows he'd take his life in his hands if he did try anything."

Joss laughs. "Oh, yeah."

Leaving them, I return to Seth, and we head along the dimly lit hallway, past the walls covered in local landscape paintings, towards the large entrance hall. Seth hunches over, hands in his pockets as he stares at the ground.

"The carpet is moving," he mutters.

I look down too, at the circular gold pattern against the burgundy. "I hope you're not going to vomit."

Seth doesn't speak again until we break out into the frosty evening. He draws in a lungful of air. "Thank fuck for that."

I cross my arms around my body to keep warm and watch the guy stumble backwards and sit on a wall. He grips the bricks and stares at the ground.

"I need to leave, Vee," he mumbles.

"If you want, I can make sure you get back to the room safely. Sleep this off, and hopefully, you'll be okay tomorrow."

"No," he says to the ground. "You need to help me get away from them. I can't do this anymore."

"I can't do that, and I don't think you should try, Seth. You've seen what's out there."

He looks up and removes his glasses, then rubs his nose. "But that's exactly why, because it's worse here! Everywhere you go shit happens to you all. I want to take my chances somewhere else in case I get caught in the crossfire. If you want to come with me, I can help you too."

I perch on the cold brick beside him. "We went through this. I'm not going anywhere. You've seen I belong with the guys."

"You all keep saying this, but the whole set up is weird, Vee. I'm scared for you. The things they do, and the way they share you, and—"

"Whoa. Stop there. Nobody 'shares' me. In case you hadn't noticed, I'm the one who calls the shots. None of them would touch me without consent."

"Even my dickhead chaperone?" He places his glasses back on. "I said right from the start, I don't trust him. He's violent. Volatile."

"Xander or Ewan?" I say.

"Both. And that 'Four Horsemen' crap they spout. I don't know how they kill as efficiently as they do, but it's not magic. It's dangerous."

I cross my legs and look across the fields to the dimly lit buildings nearby, the sounds from the party distant in the building behind. The naked sky offers no protection against the cold, and the moon shines bright. How would I expect my logical friend to do anything apart from look for scientific answers?

"You saw the demons," I say. "You know something attacked you that wasn't human."

He sits up and looks at the sky. "I don't know what to

think. I'm leaning towards military weapons, robotics, that shit."

"Which is as far-fetched as vampires and demons, really. Why believe one and not the other?"

Seth hiccups. "Okay. Whatever. But do *you* trust them?"

"Yes."

"And they trust you? Because I don't think they do. I've heard them talk about you."

I straighten. "What do you mean?"

"I don't know. I don't understand a lot of what they discuss. The hacker guy. He keeps his distance, doesn't he? I know why."

My stomach lurches. "Why? What did he say?"

"Him and Xander. I heard them talking about the trouble you cause, and how they're worried you'll destroy them."

"They wouldn't say that!" But my mind harks back to Xander's accusation on the night he discovered the secrets I kept about the Warehouse. Is he still harbouring that?

I lower my voice. "Who said I'd destroy them?"

"They both did. They want to test you, but I didn't catch how. Vee, seriously, don't trust them. What if they hurt you?"

"They can't. They won't."

"Just saying. Be careful. I know you have the measure of Xander, but Ewan... he's weirder."

I laugh lightly. "They're all weird."

"Yeah, but the things he said about you..." Seth trails off.

"What?" I demand. "What did he say?"

Seth wrings his hands together and stares into the snow stretching across the front lawns, face impassive.

"Seth?"

"That he wouldn't allow you to destroy them all; that he'd destroy you first." Seth's voice is low, and his hands shake. "*Now* do you understand why I'm scared for you? For us?"

I run both hands across my head, heart racing as I deny his words. This isn't true. It can't be. I would pick up from Ewan if he felt that about me.

But doubt creeps in. I can't detect any lies from Seth. Not one word.

"Xander feels he's lost against you, because you've trapped him somehow, and Ewan doesn't want to give you the chance. Seriously, these guys aren't normal."

"We know that," I snap, "and I think you misheard. The guys want us all united—to be stronger together."

"Please think about what I'm saying," says Seth. "Open your eyes."

"You're drunk," I reply. "Why cause trouble?"

Seth stands, unsteady on his feet. "I'm not trying to cause trouble. I'm trying to persuade you why we should leave. We can take one of their cars. Go now. Vee, please." He takes my hand between his cool ones. "I've watched people I know die. I don't want to see you hurt."

"I won't get hurt."

"How can you be so sure?" He looks back, unblinking. "How do you know?"

I pull my hands away and stand. "Seth. Stop this."

Footsteps approach along the stone path behind, and I glance around. A couple, hand in hand, pass by. I flinch in surprise as he puts both hands on my face, his voice and look earnest. "Vee. Please listen to me. Help me. Help us."

"Seth! Stop this!" My voice projects around us, and from the corner of my eye, I see a figure dressed in a dark coloured suit emerge from the shadows. Ewan seizes Seth's arm and drags him away.

"You okay, Vee?" Ewan asks, Seth's arm in a firm grip. "What's he doing?"

"He's drunk," I reply.

"And hitting on you? Not a smart move, dude." Ewan's voice drops to a growl.

"Why? Because you all own her?" laughs out Seth.

"Ewan!" I shout as I sense a flood of anger heading through him. "And Seth, I think you've said enough."

Ewan shoves Seth away from him, and Seth brushes at his suit sleeves.

"I think I need to sleep," Seth mumbles.

"This is a fucking joke," snaps Ewan. "We're here to watch what's happening. There's bloody demons here, and a possible fae plot, and we spend time chasing after the moronic human."

"Take him back to the rooms," I suggest.

"He's supposed to stay with us. Xander wants—"

"Xander," interrupts Seth as he walks off with a slight stagger. "Why do you all listen to him? Don't you ever think for yourselves?"

Ewan snaps his head around and calls, "If I don't agree with him, yes."

"The guy calls the shots, and you all do what he says. 'Yes, Xander. No, Xander. Whatever you say, psycho Xander.'"

Seth, shut up.

Ewan strides to catch up with Seth. "Yeah? Why don't you tell me more about Casey? And your friends? Why didn't whoever killed them also kill you?"

Seth stops and tips his head to look at Ewan. "Thanks. That's just the reminder I need. I can be frogmarched around by a bunch of murderous mad men, or risk life on my own running from a different bunch of maniacs. Awesome."

Seth turns towards the coach house building again and forges forward with a drunken gait.

"He's the most ungrateful arsehole," mutters Ewan.

My system remains filled with confusion and anger at Seth's words. Why would Ewan say those things about me? "I'll go back with him."

Ewan grabs my wrist as I make to follow. "We both will. I'm not leaving you on your own with him."

"I won't be with him, just in the same building. Go back to Joss."

"No fucking way. Come on." Ewan stomps ahead, and I grit my teeth.

Seth wants to leave, but I doubt he'd stagger drunk through a Scottish estate, miles from the nearest town, in freezing November temperatures. I don't rate his survivalist skills.

21

*V*EE

I walk after the two guys, skin covered in goose bumps. Bloody good thing we're halfway there because I'm losing sensation in my hands. Seth heads straight for his room and slams the door before either of us can follow him.

Ewan stares as the wood almost hits his face.

"Are you going to stand outside as his sentry?" I ask as I unlock the door to my room.

Ewan looks between the two rooms and pushes hair from his face. "What are you doing?"

"Heading to bed. Why? Do you think you need to guard me too?"

"Huh?"

I close my eyes and rub my temples. I'm not drunk, but there's enough in my system for me to spill out what Seth told me if I don't keep my mouth shut.

"Doesn't matter. I'll see you in the morning."

"What's wrong, Vee?"

"I'm just struggling a bit too. Feeling on the outside." I bite back saying anymore.

He places his hand on the door to stop me closing it. "Why do you feel on the outside? Has Xander been saying stupid shit again?"

"It doesn't matter, Ewan. Good night."

I turn and walk into the darkened room. As I head to the nightstand and switch on the light, the door clicks closed behind me.

Ewan's large frame takes up the doorway, face unclear in the dim. "You know you can talk to me if you need to."

"Can I?" I place down my handbag and kick off my shoes. "You're hard to talk to. Even harder than Xander, in a way."

"What way?"

"At least he shouts his thoughts and feelings at me, instead of harbouring whatever ones you do."

"What the hell are you talking about, Vee?"

I walk towards him. "The day after I fooled around with the guys in the snow, you said we were going to talk, so talk."

"Whoa. Okay." Ewan pushes hair from his face. "Are you pissed off with me over what just happened with Seth? Sorry, but I just can't trust him, and I wish you'd open your eyes."

"No." I take a ragged breath. "Not that."

"Then what? Why this sudden change in attitude? You seemed relaxed and happy around us before."

The words spill from my mouth before I can stop them. "Do you want to destroy me?"

Ewan steps back and looks at me as if I've punched him in the face. "What?" His voice is low, barely a whisper. "What the fuck makes you think I want to... Vee, that's insane."

"Is it? You told me from the start I'd cause problems. You've seen and told me how I come between you all."

"Wrong. We all fight sometimes. There're parts of each of us that could destroy our group, but we deal with conflict." He wipes a hand across his face. "It bloody hurts you saying this to me, Vee. I'm trying to protect you."

"What from? You think because I have this connection to all of you that I'll become too strong and kill you all?"

"Where's this crazy idea come from?" His mouth parts. "It's him, isn't it? Seth! The fucking devious... He's gone too far."

As Ewan spins to leave, I call out, 'The things he said weren't lies, Ewan."

The awkward tension following us recently switches, and an angry undercurrent starts as our words harshen.

"What things?" He turns back to me.

"You and Xander want me gone. Destroyed. You don't trust me." All of Seth's words rush out, at the same time reinforcing in my mind one thing: *Seth wasn't lying.*

"No. He *is* lying. I have *never* said that. It's the opposite of what I want." He attempts to take my arm, and I step back.

"How can he lie? I would know!" I choke on the words, and the realisation Seth could be right. That I'm dangerous. That they don't trust me.

"Vee. How could I want to destroy you? I love you."

I begin to tell him he's lying, but can't. The confusion and hurt on Ewan's face isn't a lie, and neither is his admission. I don't move when he approaches me and holds my face hard in both large palms. Tears well in my eyes, building with the confusion causing the pressure in my head.

His breaths come in short bursts as he studies my face. "I can give you bullshit excuses about being scared what might happen to the five of us if we had sex, but that's not the only reason." His hands are rough against my skin, his words spoken in a desperate earnestness. "You told me you didn't want to feel anything. You'd pulled all these emotions I was struggling to deal with out of me, then threw them back in my face. I thought you hurt me that evening, but saying these things now is worse, Vee... How can you think this?"

A tear escapes my eye and trails onto Ewan's hand. He looks at his fingers in alarm. "I don't know how Seth has managed to lie to you, but he has. Believe me."

My throat thickens and head pounds because the words coming from Ewan's mouth aren't lies either. What the fuck is happening here? His face holds a truth I wish I'd never doubted. Did I doubt myself and that's why I believed Seth?

"Then we need to find out how Seth could lie to me."

"Oh yeah, wait until I get my hands on that fucker."

I wipe my face with the back of a hand and smile weakly. "Not now, Ewan. We need to talk. We've left it long enough."

Ewan slides his hand into my hair, thumb circling the nape of my neck and sending a shiver through me. "I don't want to destroy you, Vee. I want to love you—to have you love me. But for the first time the future frightens me, and it's holding me back."

"Why?"

"Because you came from nowhere, what happens if you leave once you've fulfilled whatever you're here to do? I couldn't cope if..." He inhales sharply and rests his forehead on mine. "If you left again, you would tear me apart. It would destroy me."

"I'm not going anywhere," I whisper.

Ewan tightens his grip on my hair, forehead still on mine. We're together, but he's still so far, no longer looking into my eyes. "How can you be sure?"

I pull away and move his face, forcing him to look at me. "Because the four of you complete me, and I don't just mean because of the powers. We're stronger together, and I'm stronger because of you all. I love you deeply, Ewan. This between us all is so much more than supernatural connections. You guys will do anything to keep me safe, and I will kill anybody who tries to come between us."

His eyes widen. "Whoa. Vee."

The words shock me too, but they're wired into me somehow.

"You'd do the same, for any of us," I reply.

"I guess."

I shake my head at his hesitancy. "It's too late for anybody to do anything now. How could they destroy someone who holds every single power each Horseman has? Why else would people search for me and want to stop me being with you?""

Ewan's eyes meet mine, and we share the same thought. Do I? Because I don't share Heath's life-giving, and I've never experienced Ewan's. I don't think my computer skills are the power he shares with me.

We both know there's only one way we can discover if I can.

"I belong here, with all of you. I'm part of you all, and nothing could ever tear us apart now we're together. Nothing."

Ewan runs his finger along my cheek, his concerned eyes darkening with an intent that flips my stomach. All I want is his lips and his hands on me, to be in his arms tonight and feel the love he told me he's holding back. Forget Seth. Forget demons. Forget the craziness outside this room. Right now, this needs to be about us.

"I can prove everything I'm telling you, Vee," he says hoarsely. "I want to so fucking much."

Ewan's eyes burn with a new fervour, and I move my mouth to reach his. He responds with a sudden and engulfing kiss, his tongue parting my lips as he kisses me deeply.

The intense passion overtakes me in seconds, and I grip his head so he can't pull away. Ewan doesn't need persuading, kissing me harder, scruff scratching my cheek. His taste and scent intoxicate me, and I shake as he circles his arms around my waist, holding me to him. I tear my mouth away to catch my breath, and Ewan shifts his attention to my neck, kissing and nipping my skin.

His hands slide along my leg, pushing beneath my dress until he reaches my ass, and digs his fingers into the skin as he holds my hips against his. His arousal pushes against me, and the ache between my legs grows at his touch. The movement of his lips on mine travels into every nerve ending, my body aching for him. Ewan pushes my dress higher, and right now all I want is the flimsy material between us gone.

I reach behind me, attempting to pull at the zip and failing. Ewan rests his head on my shoulder, hot breath against my face as he pushes my hand away to pull. He tugs but the zip doesn't move, then pulls harder.

"Don't tear my dress! I need this for tomorrow."

"Fine." In a swift movement, Ewan seizes hold of me and pushes backwards so I fall onto the bed, my hair splaying across the sheets.

The crumpled sheets are cool against my hot skin as Ewan presses himself onto me, and his cotton shirt brushes my peaked nipples. I can't move, as our limbs tangle and mouths lock. He kneels and settles between my legs, pushing my dress to my waist, and himself against me. As Ewan's mouth hungrily claims mine, his hands move to my leg again, but this time when he pushes his hand up my thigh, he doesn't stop. The rough passion shocks and arouses me, as he gives in to his lust.

Beneath his hands and mouth, I disintegrate into pleasure, digging my nails into Ewan's back to keep myself grounded, trembling. I shuffle backwards onto the bed and pull Ewan by the shirt, wanting his body covering mine. He slides his hand to the zip again, and as he pulls hard, I hear the material rip.

"Ewan!"

"Don't care." He pulls the straps down my shoulders and nips my skin from my earlobe to my neck as he pushes the material down exposing my breasts swelling against my lace bra. With both hands he yanks at the material, watching with heavy breaths as he reveals more of my skin. I wriggle so he can pull away my dress. He looks down, and heat grazes my skin as he strokes my belly, teasingly playing with the edge of my panties, soaking up the sight of me.

"I can't believe I've waited this long to see you naked." Before I can catch my breath, he pulls at my panties too, dragging them from my legs to the floor, my bra following shortly after.

Ewan stands and grabs his shirt between the shoulder blades, the powerful muscles in his arms flexing as he does. I inhale sharply as I take in the sight of him; at the tattoos I ached to trace with my fingers; the broad chest he's held me against in the past. As I stare, he kicks off his shoes and unbuttons his trousers, eyes on mine, and they drop to the floor next to his shirt.

Wow. Ewan. Naked. Finally. Six-foot-plus of solid muscle, ink etched across his arms and torso. The dim light from the small lamp highlights every inch of his sculpted physique, from the contours of his chest and tight abs to the powerful arms and shoulders.

I barely get a chance to soak in the sight before Ewan kneels on the floor. He reaches out a hand and runs his hands across my skin, tracing the mount of my breasts, rough thumb brushing my nipples. Mouth parted, breath coming quicker, Ewan watches as he maps my skin with his fingertips. I tense, anticipating his touch as he runs his fingers along my belly and downwards.

Without a word, Ewan drags me roughly toward him by the ankles. He parts my legs, and he kisses his way from my calf upwards, his stubbled cheek rough against my thigh. Strong hands slide beneath my ass and pull me upwards, and I jolt at the sensation as his tongue slides along my flesh.

I grip the edge of the sheets and bite back the groan as Ewan teases me with soft strokes of his tongue. Ever since that first night in the kitchen, I've dreamed of being with Ewan again. The frustration built from wanting his hands and mouth on me finally releases as the pleasure coils deep inside and the shaking intensifies. In moments, he has me spiralling high; and when Ewan slips a finger inside me again, I fight against crying out.

The pressure builds, and I can't decide whether to move my shaking self away or give in to the inevitable. The choice isn't mine, as Ewan holds me to him, his fingers digging into my backside as he moves his fingers and tongue harder. Shivers run along my spine over and over as he sucks on my clit, and his scruff scrapes against me as he moves his face against my sensitive flesh. I let go, pushing into him, and grasping his hair as I chase the stars. They blind me as the orgasm hits; sudden and intense.

When I open them again, Ewan's arms are either side of me, as he looks down, eyes burning with a passion to match mine. His smile grows as he looks down at the panting mess he's made of me. He wipes his face with the back of his hand and sits on his haunches, chest rising and falling rapidly.

"Are we good?" he asks, voice hoarse.

"What?" Realisation dawns. "Ewan! Are you avoiding sex with me still?"

Ewan takes a shuddering breath and laughs. He's bloody teasing me. I launch myself forward and, taking him by surprise, Ewan falls backwards onto the carpet. The sheets from the bed drop to the floor next to us. I straddle him, his cock pushing against my stomach instead. I mash my mouth with his, gripping his head in both hands. The distraction works, and he moves his hand from the floor to hold my face and kiss me back, sinking onto the carpet. He stops and holds my cheeks, eyes searching my face.

"Let go, Ewan," I say. "You always promised me next time you wouldn't hold back."

"No way am I holding back. Not with you like that. Fuck, Vee." He pants out the words as I slide him against my slick pussy.

Ewan lets go of my hair and in a swift move tips me over onto the sheets covering the carpet. I gasp as my back hits the floor. Pinioning my hands back over my head with one hand, he pushes my legs open with his knee. All I'm aware of is the tip of him resting against my sensitive flesh, and I shift my hips, desperate for Ewan to fill me.

Something passes between us as his darkened gaze meets mine; the understanding that we're about to cross a line and we don't know where we'll be once we do. I open my mouth to tell him not to stop, and not to be pulled back by doubts.

But Ewan's beyond thinking.

I gasp as he thrusts into me hard then stops, kissing me again, and forcing my mouth open to accept his tongue. I grip his shoulders, fingers digging into the knotted muscle, and lock my legs around his waist; I fit tightly around him but want him closer. Ewan pulls his head away and takes a deep breath. He withdraws slowly, watching my face as he runs his fingers along my lips.

"You feel so fucking good," he says, voice hoarse.

Ewan pushes into me again and again, faster and faster, lust darkening his expression, eyes combing every inch of me as he maintains the rhythm. The ebbing pleasure resurges and I push against Ewan's hips, matching his movements. He rocks his hips against me driving us closer to what we both reach out for.

Mouth parted and eyes closed, Ewan gathers pace, reaching for his release too. The lightning trips along my spine again and into my limbs once more, shocking me back to the black behind my eyes.

I knew something would happen once I fell away from myself and into this moment with Ewan. But this is different to the other guys: light doesn't blind us; there's no lightbulb shattering; no channelled emotions. The disease and infection Ewan feared he'd create doesn't happen.

Yet with Ewan, something greater takes hold.

Ewan stares down at me in concern as I gasp for breath, the orgasm still shaking through but joined by something stronger. A new power courses through my veins, burning across my skin. A stinging sensation coils around my body, beginning in the centre of my chest, and grips me with a pain I resist and relish at the same time.

As my pleasure-blackened senses sharpen and the ache intensifies. I cry out, shaking and the perspiration growing from the pain. The room seems to shrink, and I'm pulled into myself, away from the world, away from Ewan, as the constricting room suffocates me.

I stare upwards into a blurred world, and no longer see Ewan's face.

"Vee?" Ewan's voice is distant and not part of my world.

I push him, and he moves away from me. The room shimmers and a void resembling a night sky with no stars, forms in the corner of the room. I shuffle back on the bed, convinced the shadows will swallow me.

"Ewan!"

As I stare into the black, a pinprick of light forms in the centre of the void, growing larger and rushing closer until a huge ball of blinding light breaks through. I scream as the pure energy flies across the room and hits me in the chest.

The pain immediately stops, and my trembling body jerks before a new power rushes in. I close my eyes and images flood into my mind. A darkness covers the sky, the world around me on fire, acrid smoke filling my lungs. I suck in a huge breath as, in my vision, I turn in a slow circle and stare at the eerie silence in the destruction around me. This is a city. Or it was. Buildings no longer stand, people no longer walk by. Everything is lost in a thick smoky haze.

The outline of a dark figure stands nearby, made from the same starless void where the light that hit me came from. He holds a body in his hands and tosses it to one side as if it were a doll and I cry out. The Four Horsemen lie on the ground, at his feet.

I snap my eyes open in terror and grip at Ewan's hand, who's speaking but I can't hear a word. Even holding him doesn't ground me, I'm in this room but no longer feel as if I'm here.

I shudder at the sense that, somewhere in the world, this evil exists and is ready to unleash. I have to find who I saw and stop the horror he intends to bring.

Nausea sweeps over me joined by a wave of panic. What do I do now?

22

*E*WAN

*V*ee pulls away and grabs clothes slung over a nearby chair, almost falling over as she pulls her jeans on. I prop myself up on the bed, and stare in disbelief.

"Vee?"

She pulls on and fastens her bra, then grabs a shirt, barely registering me.

"What's wrong?" I sit. "What happened?" I reach out to her, but she doesn't respond.

I fucking knew this would happen. Nobody listened when I said our union would change her. That giving in to the all-consuming need for sex with Vee, to give my heart and soul to her would transform the girl she is into something else.

The incredible, mind-shattering moment we looked into each other's eyes, and I saw my love reflected in hers, dropped away as they filled with terror. At first, I thought I'd hurt her, and then she filled me with fear that something was in the room with us.

The only thing I could see was the girl I love struggling. Lost. In pain.

And now this. Something isn't right.

"I need to go." Her voice is low, different, and when Vee looks around it's as if she sees right through me.

"Go where? Back to the party?"

She stares back into the corner of the room, to the space she was mesmerised by a few moments ago, eyes filled with terror again. "I can't... I need to get out."

"Where? Vee, what the hell is wrong?"

Holding her temples with her forefingers, Vee stares straight ahead face paler than I've seen before. "I don't know. I just... I feel sick. I need air."

I jump from the bed and drag my jeans on too, as Vee opens the room door. "Look, wait for—"

The door slams behind her before I can slip my boots on to follow.

What the hell?

What the fuck have I done?

Is this my worst fears realised?

Jacket half-on, I stagger from the room, boots half-laced, desperate to catch up with her before she does god knows what.

Because the girl who walked out of this room is not the one who I opened up to and gave myself to. It's as if somebody or something replaced her and that fucking terrifies me.

The opposite door opens and Seth stands wide-eyed, fully clothed.

"What did you do?" he hisses.

I snap my head back. "None of your business, mate." I need to catch Vee and make sure she's okay.

"Did you argue? I heard you argue. Is that why she walked away?" I stare at his reddening face. "Please tell me that's the reason, and that you didn't—"

"Assault her? Is that what you're about to say?" I step forward, the suggestion I'd ever hurt Vee building anger in my belly. "I would never touch her without consent."

He flicks a gaze over me and narrows his eyes. "Did it happen?"

"Did what happen?"

He lowers his voice. "You and her. Did you screw her?"

Bad move. I grab Seth's jacket in both hands and drag his face close to mine. His breath stinks of the alcohol that's caused this issue. "Watch your mouth."

"You have!" He tears at my fingers. "Do you know what you've done, you fucking idiot?"

Seth's face reddens, drunken eyes suddenly switching to a glittering anger, and I drop his collar and stand back as he drags fingernails across my hands.

"Fuck!" Seth yells, his voice echoing along the small hallway. He turns his back and walks away from me hands behind his head, elbows at right angles. "Fuck!"

Yeah, fuck this weirdo; I need to find Vee. Now. I turn away and pick up my pace to leave.

"Don't you walk away from me!" Seth spits.

I choke a laugh and turn back. "Mate, seriously, you're lucky I'm not punching you to the ground for what you just said. I need to find Vee. I'll deal with you later."

Seth's expression shifts, transforming into an anger that makes his features unrecognisable. I've seen many things in Seth's expression I think the others missed, but never a shaking fury to match Xander's. There's no sign of the pathetic, drunk guy I left in his room earlier.

"Deal with me?" Seth shouts. "You have no fucking chance of dealing with me. None of you morons do."

I ready a retort, unprepared for his next move. Seth strides over and shoves me in the chest with both hands. The world blurs and I find myself halfway along the hallway, landing heavily on my backside, as he hits me like a truck.

What the fuck?

I push my arms behind me attempting to sit, and Seth strides over. Without pausing, he kicks me in the stomach with an unnatural force and the pain screams through my body. "You shouldn't have done that! You've fucked up everything!"

I struggle to breathe after the blow and can't move. "What the fuck do you think you're doing?" *And how?*

Seth sneers down, and I attempt to tackle him to the ground, arms around his legs, but he slips through them like the snake he is. I drag myself to my feet and support myself against the wall, doubling over as I take painful breaths. I've been kicked before, many times, but this feels like he's pummelled my insides. "I knew it," I gasp. "I fucking knew you were trouble."

I study him. He's the same man, the same body, but something's wrong. The brute force he hit me with isn't human, nor is the person looking at me through those eyes. Hell, I've looked into enough eyes in my time here to know when something isn't human, and there's a hollow darkness; one I've not seen before.

I take a deep breath and wince. "What are you? How did you hit me that hard?"

Seth leans in and places his face close to mine. "I guess I

don't know my own strength." Then, right in my face, he gives the sly smile, the one I see when nobody else does. "Like Xander, if I lose my temper things don't go so well for the people around me."

"Are you a demon? How come Joss and Vee didn't know?"

Seth's face sours. "Please. I'm nothing like those low lives." He pulls away. "One thing I'm in total agreement with is demon scum shouldn't be in this world."

I don't scare easily. I've stared down enough demons to see them as part of my job, but whatever stands in front of me now projects an energy that fills the corridor and sucks oxygen from the room. His eyes blacken and an energy shimmers around him to match the light I see around Vee sometimes.

Is he suffocating me? Or is my tight chest and struggle breathing genuine fear? I steady myself on the wall and stare back. The weak human I suspected worked for someone, who I swore I could take out, isn't even human. I don't know what the hell he is, but this is no demon.

"What are you then? Fae?"

Seth rests against the wall next to me, then holds out his palms towards me, but this is no gesture of surrender. I focus on gathering my strength to move as I watch the space in front of him blacken, as if somebody dragged the light and air away, until all that remains resembles a dark, starless sky.

He stares at the void. "Nope. There's only one person in this world more powerful than me, and she just walked out of the door. And that's really fucking inconvenient for me."

I shuffle back as fast as I can as he turns his palms in my direction. The dark space grows around us both, obliterating everything as if somebody scrawled out the world with a black marker pen.

Holy shit.

Seth drops his hands with a satisfied look as he laughs at my fear, and the consuming darkness snaps away too. "I'd kill you, but there's no point until I've killed your friend Death and, of course, made sure Vee never fulfils the destiny they gave her."

Still doubled over, I continue to edge back along the wall, but the pain won't stop spreading through. I bow my head and concentrate on summoning energy I'm shocked I don't have.

"What happened to her?"

"You fucked her and now you've fucked things up for me." He rubs his temples. "I guess I'd better bring forward my plans now."

His words seethe anger through me, and I look upwards and picture how I could attack him. Do I have the power?

"Don't even think about it, Ewan. Believe me, you'd wish you could die if I really hurt you." His glittering black eyes meet mine again. "I'm saving that fun. I cannot *wait* to take down that condescending arsehole, War. That will be the highlight of the show, and you can be the encore."

I remain slumped against the wall, unable to move further.

Seth grabs my hair and yanks my head upwards, face in mine again. "I guess this is a tender goodbye for now. Shame this happened before Syv found what I needed and the time was right."

"Get the fuck off me," I snarl.

"You were very intuitive, by the way, which surprised me because I thought you were incapable of thinking for yourself." Seth pats me on the cheek. "Clever boy, you almost figured me out."

He releases my hair and steps back, and I stare as he closes his eyes, and the void I saw before grows around him. The space where Seth stood empties as his figure disintegrates and merges with the darkness.

I slump back to the floor, gripping my stomach, filled with a fear, but not only for myself.

What the hell is he?

23

X ANDER

eath rests against the wall, to the left of a door, knife in hand. I rest against the right-hand side, door between us.

We tracked Logan and Breanna through the house. They didn't go far, downstairs, to the right of the conference room where Alasdair gave his introduction earlier, and down an opposite hallway. We followed at a distance until they walked into the room in front of us now. The situation is ridiculous. I'm ninety percent sure they knew we were behind them—as planned.

Heath nods, a silent signal that we enter and face down whatever and whoever is inside. At moments like this, I always feel a weird surge of anticipation, a build-up to dealing with the unknown on the other side of a door or around a corner. This is the closest I get to experiencing rawer human reactions, or they were until I met Vee.

Pulling my knife too, I yank open the door and step in, Heath by my side, and immediately scan the room for which threat to take out first.

Two men and a woman sit around a large conference table, carafes of water in front of them, alongside glasses, half-full. Each sits with arms on the table in front, talking, as if taking part in a company meeting.

The guy sitting in the centre holds up a hand to stop the others talking.

Alasdair.

Then I focus on the man beside him.

Logan.

Next to him, Breanna.

Heath drops his knife to the floor, and as my triggered power launches strength into every muscle, I hear the familiar crackle that comes with his conjured power. Easy. We do this, help Alasdair, and leave.

"Boys, please. Stand down. I'm not about to do anything."

I cock my head. Alasdair sounds different. The Scottish accent is missing and as he smiles back, his eyes transform into pure black, with an orange slit resembling a cat's eye. Something shudders through my body and into my soul.

There's only one entity I know who has eyes like this.

I've met this demon before. Not occupying this body, but in another I almost destroyed, when he escaped before I had a chance to finish the job.

In the past, we downplayed who this powerful demon is, and his strength, by nicknaming him the Big Bad. We've battled him once, as the four of us, and after an exhausting fight taking out his demon protectors, he escaped. He's the centre of the Order, who draws on his power to create more demons when we slay others. His power isn't infinite, and he's working to get his boss—whoever he is—into the world from beyond the portals.

Our lives are one big game of cat and mouse, where we find and lose him over and over.

As the Order's influence grows throughout government and industry, our ability to keep up with him drops away.

This is who I suspect left us the message on the car and who's been killing the humans—and us.

This is Ripley, the Moriarty to our Sherlock selves.

He stands and spreads his arms out in greeting. "I won't do anything untoward, although I owe you a death after what happened the last time we met. You killed some of my best."

"Ripley?" I ask to confirm.

"The same."

How fucked are we? If I'd had any suspicions this is what we were walking into, I would've found the other guys first.

Heath swears under his breath, and suddenly our pathetic weapons are pointless.

"Unusual for you to be out of your ivory tower and unprotected," I snap. "Where are your little minions?" I point at Breanna. "One won't do you much good."

Breanna's red painted lips broaden into a smile. "I'm not just any demon, sweetheart."

Ripley sighs. "I know. I've chosen a new profile. Just recently actually." He blinks back to his human eyes and gestures at himself. "Not as strong as I'd like, but he's a good looking vessel and not so bad for his age." I frown at him, so he turns to Breanna. "Don't you think?"

They share a laugh, and I bristle.

"I like to keep my identity well hidden because some are better at finding me than you four idiots are. I currently need to shift from host to host almost daily. It's exhausting, but I've managed to stay safe. The problem is I have to choose less than perfect specimens to hold me."

I study him. Yeah, the guy usually chooses playboy types, or people with influence. Those who can get him what he wants, or allow him close to plenty of people to corrupt. "And kill them daily?"

"I'm still Alasdair. Well, kind of. He's still in here. I'm being nice and didn't eradicate him first." He gives another smile. "The guy has such beautifully altruistic motives, how could I kill him? He's been so helpful too, even before he lent me his body." He gestures at the seat opposite. "Sit."

"I'd rather stand, thanks," Heath replies.

Ripley shrugs. "But how can we have a discussion if you won't join in our meeting?"

I switch to glare at Logan. "Does Portia know you're here?"

Logan raises a brow. "What do you think?"

"So you're working with him?" I jab a finger at Ripley. "I had my suspicions! All that shit you said about Vee."

He shakes his head. "I'm not taking those words back, and I have plenty more to tell you, should you want to listen."

"What's the deal?" interrupts Heath. "Why are you with the Order?"

Ripley sits back in his seat and folds his arms on the table. "Because we need to help each other. Portia won't listen to Logan's suggestions that she forms an alliance with us. We're hoping you'll be more sensible."

"Sensible?" I laugh. "A demon tried to kill Portia, remember? I think that *might* just've put her off."

"Not one of mine," replies Alasdair.

"Oh sure, you never attack fae. Not your style." I sneer at him.

"Not this time. The attack was planned by somebody intending to push us and the fae further apart. Somebody had too much influence over a small group of demons and had whispered too many promises. That group were stupid, and they're gone."

"I don't believe you."

"It's true," says Logan. "And I know things have been orchestrated against you too. Danger surrounds you all."

I pull myself to full height. "Are you talking about Vee? Because if you're threatening her, you'll have to come through me first."

The arsehole fae laughs at me. If the table wasn't between us, I'd show him exactly what I think about him betraying his race.

Ripley bangs a hand on the table. "We're short of time. Let's have the conversation and then these *gentlemen* can decide what to do. Sit."

I cross my arms. "No. Whatever trick you're trying to pull won't work. If you're involved with Nova Pharm, you'll know about the humans investigating your activities. You identified them and killed them. Why? What did they uncover?"

"Nothing. Sit." His voice is firmer, but no self-titled demon overlord tells me what to do. "Or not. Really, War, you need to listen."

"To you?" I laugh harshly. "Heath? Do we stay? Or leave and figure out a way to take these guys out."

I don't take my eyes from Ripley's, whose lips curl in amusement. "Listen to me."

"Why?"

"Because I have the answer to all your questions. I've had people watching what's been happening to you. I've seen you run around in circles chasing your tails, completely oblivious." He pauses. "I've also watched your Fifth arrive, and this worries me. But one thing at a time."

"Yeah, we've come across your attempts to kill us. How long until you realise a Horseman's death is never permanent?"

"Me?" He touches his chest in mock horror. "I haven't tried to kill you. Currently, it isn't in my interests to piss you off."

I turn my attention to Logan. "You? Was it you trying to divide our alliance with Portia? With each other?"

He watches me in his haughty way. "I don't trust any outside the fae—you or them—but somebody needs to take charge here. Portia's in denial and won't listen when I tell her darker forces are at work."

"Darker than him?" I point at Ripley. "You know he kills humans and fae in his quest to overthrow the world?"

"Please, Alexander, don't be so dramatic."

"Xander," I growl. "So you deny you're wrapping your evil tendrils around every important part of human society and paving the way for your demon leader to breach the portal?"

"Again, far too simplistic and not the most important thing on my agenda right now."

"So what is? Joining Logan to overthrow Portia and get your claws into the fae? Attempting to be rid if us? We won't let that happen."

"Believe me, once this larger threat is dealt with, I'll be back to my usual activities, but if this continues, none of us will survive."

"This?"

"Chaos," puts in Logan.

"And what's causing the chaos? Normally it's you, Ripley."

"No. Chaos." Logan straightens. "We are dealing with

something much more powerful than Ripley, or anything else that has threatened the world before. That's why I'm working with him."

Ripley nods in agreement. "Yes. This new threat predates our arrival here and he has no interest in anything apart from destroying the world he created."

I blink. "Who? Is this Biblical stories again? Are you talking about God?"

"No, we're talking about Chaos. He's an old god, not yours. He didn't just create the world, he *is* the world. This entity is the explosive chaos that began everything in the universe. Compared to him, your God is a toddler."

"I don't have a God," I reply.

"Of course you don't." Ripley smiles sweetly.

I glance at Heath as he pulls out a chair and sits. "Are you saying something is in this world who wants to end it? Like an—"

"Apocalypse?" interrupts Logan.

"How?"

"By opening every portal at once and allowing each race living in the realms behind them to enter this world. Chaos will unleash one hell of a war. The human population will be destroyed, cities razed, the whole planet polluted and decimated to suit the victor's needs. Then, Chaos will take hold and reign. There will be no portals, no universe, nothing, just his dark power looking over the devastation left."

I shake my head at Logan's words, despite the growing anxiety gripping my chest. "Bullshit."

"I think you believe us. You have to admit what you've fought recently is harder than anything I've been able to throw at you." He taps his fingers on the table. "Unfortunately."

"You're not responsible for what happened to Ewan? Joss?" I ask.

Ripley smiles. "No. If I was, I would've used that to my advantage long before now. You know that."

"Where is Chaos?" asks Heath. "How do we fight him?"

I stare at Heath. "You don't believe them do you? This is a trick. Is this because you want Vee? Is it all to do with her?"

"I think this is why she's here. Without her, we don't stand a chance. If she reaches full power, Chaos doesn't stand a chance," Ripley replies.

"We hope," adds Logan.

"How?"

"My friend Breanna has a gift for translating old texts." Ripley gestures at her. "The problem is, the Collector has many of them, including the book with the runes and descriptions of what they do and how they operate. We need all the information and we only have half. Breanna could translate them for us."

"And the Collector won't let you close?" asks Heath.

"No."

"Have you spoken to him about Chaos? About what it means for the world?"

"Not yet. He would never speak to me, but Logan tried. The Collector refuses to speak to the other fae. He's tired of being badgered," says Ripley.

"Plus an email, 'by the way did you know an Old God intends to destroy the world' probably wouldn't get much response either," puts in Breanna with a smile.

"So what do you want? For us and Vee to find this Chaos and kill him? Is this why you've created this ridiculous situation, thinking you have us trapped? And why Nova Pharm? Why are you connecting yourself to them?"

"Because Chaos is tracking me, and I wanted to bring

him out into the open. So far, we have little idea who he is, but I involved myself in Nova Pharm and left clues. When somebody began digging around, and we realised it wasn't you, we watched and waited."

"And?"

"Nothing concrete yet."

I snort. "And did you kill the humans while looking for 'something concrete'?"

"No, we think he did. This god is well hidden, and he can disguise himself as anyone or anything, undetected. But his nature prevents him keeping the chaos under wraps for long. We think he maintains a strict control over his daily human life, to cage his chaos if that make sense."

"He also enjoys creating the chaos he represents," puts in Logan. "Another of his downfalls, but to our advantage because it slows his plans down."

"Yes, he's taking his time. Having fun. He's left false trails for the Horsemen, leading them to us. Chaos built distrust amongst the fae and broke down alliances."

"And now you want us to ally with *you*?" I scoff a laugh. "No way."

"Are you listening? This god can devastate the world. He's already started. It's insidious right now, as he corrupts the humans and their society better than I ever could. Next he'll start revealing to the humans the other races amongst them, and you can imagine the uh... *chaos* that will cause."

"We say 'he' but this god could equally disguise himself as a woman." Logan raps his fingers on the table. "I've told Ripley we need to consider that possibility."

I look at Heath whose confusion matches mine. Chaos. The word has appeared everywhere for us in the last few weeks, and hit around the same time Vee did.

"Are you going to tell us Vee is really Chaos?" I ask in a

hoarse voice, "Because there's no way I can believe that. Yes, we're agents of chaos in some respects, but this is crazy."

"Oh no, we think you're the solution, or I wouldn't be having this conversation," Ripley says. "You can stop him. Or at least we hope you're powerful enough together. We're hoping somebody put Truth here to help with this, but we need to find out how."

I look to Heath for an answer, what to say, but he's staring into space. "You tricked us into coming here, didn't you?" he asks in a low voice.

"Tricked? No, we needed you to bring one of the humans we believe is connected to Chaos. We've had trouble watching Seth, thanks to you." Ripley leans forwards, elbows on the table. "Since he joined the Horsemen, we've been unable to study or track him or to find out what happened to his friends. Don't you think it's a coincidence that Seth's the only one alive from the group we were watching? The ones we didn't kill, by the way."

Yes. *Fuck.*

"We needed to have this conversation too, and I doubt an invitation to meet would've helped. Now you've brought Seth to us; we can persuade him to tell us what the hell he knows and who he's working for. He's not leaving until he does. Alive or dead."

Heath shakes his head. "No. No."

I frown at my brother's response. Isn't he suspicious of Seth too? Hell, this is exactly what Ewan's been saying all along. Seth is working with someone else. Seth is not who he says.

"I think you have this all wrong," Heath continues. "Everything you've said about Chaos and how he operates, and how well hidden he is. It makes sense, Xander."

My heart rate skyrockets as Heath looks at me, and I already know what he's about to say. "I think Seth is Chaos."

Ripley chuckles. "I don't think so. Chaos is too powerful to be contained in a human that weak. He'd need somebody stronger."

"How do you know that? If he's a god, surely he can be what he wants and do what he wants. You said he created the universe; disguising himself and hiding from us isn't a big deal," Heath replies.

I drag a hand through my hair. Powerful.

How fucking powerful?

Why the fuck didn't anybody pick up that Seth isn't human?

"Heath. We need to find the others."

"And do what?" he replies.

"Make sure they're okay!" I snap. "If we're what stands between Seth... Chaos and his plans, I don't know what he's waiting for, but he could do something at any moment."

Heath silently stares ahead, massaging his temples. "This explains a lot, Xander. Seth's been dividing us—and pushing us away from Vee. Who has he clashed with the most? Ewan. Ewan, the one of us we need closer to her right now. He's distracting us, and now I'm bloody sure Vee needs Ewan to complete her powers."

"Ah. Truth." Breanna leans forward and puts her head in her hands. "Now she is a conundrum. I have information about who you are, boys, but I'm stumped on who she is."

"What do you mean?"

"Ask your companion, Famine, how he is. He's starting to remember things, which is unusual. Someone is separating the veil between your current and past selves; I think we can all guess who." She rubs her mouth with a slender finger. "I know you all have moments when this happens, but it's happening quicker this time. This will screw you over and weaken you because it will fuck with ycur heads."

"Who are you?" I growl.

"You could call me a human resources manager."

"At Nova Pharm?" asks Heath.

"Please, we can get back to this later." Ripley scratches his cheek. "We need to know— will you join with us to end this threat. We can make it mutually beneficial?"

"How?"

"Well, first we can call a ceasefire and second, well, we all want a world to live in that's in one piece."

"Ha ha, you mean the world you want to bring your demon friends to conquer? Yeah... um, no."

"Are you listening?" Ripley's voice rises. "There will be no world for any of us! Isn't that the Horsemen's whole reason for being here? You will not be able to do this alone. Not quickly enough."

I stand. "We'll manage. This must be the reason Vee is here."

"Well, you don't seem to be managing very well so far."

Heath places an arm on my sleeve. "Maybe we should listen."

I blink at him in shock. "Are you serious?"

"If Seth is Chaos, he's played us for days. If he's undetectable in human form, how the hell are we supposed to find him if he gets away? Or what if he hurts Vee?"

"Shit." I stand. "We need to deal with Seth. We'll bring him here, and between us, we'll find out who the fuck he is. What he is. Heath?"

Heath stands, but his look is panicked. "I'm telling you. He's Chaos, and if he is and knows we've discovered this, I don't think we have any chance of bringing him to anybody."

I straighten my shoulders. "I'm willing to bet Vee can."

Ripley stands and straightens his shirtsleeves. "I bloody hope so, because if she's here to help him, and not us, then we are, to put it bluntly, fucked."

I rub a hand across my face, paralysed for a moment by the shock and confusion. What is the whole story here? Our greatest enemies hold some of the information we need, and we have the help they need. The world— supernatural and human—is threatened by something nobody fully understands.

I never imagined the chaos surrounding us since Vee arrived existed in reality, and I've never imagined I'd spend ten minutes in a room with demons and see everybody survive.

The world is more screwed than I thought.

Is Vee here to help or is her arrival the beginning of the end?

To be continued

OTHER BOOKS BY LJ SWALLOW

The Four Horsemen Series
Reverse Harem Urban Fantasy
Legacy
Bound
Hunted
Guardians
Chaos
Descent
Reckoning

The Soul Ties series
New Adult Paranormal Romance/Urban Fantasy
Fated Souls: A Prequel Novella
Soul Ties
Torn Souls
Shattered Souls

Touched By The Dark
Paranormal romance/Urban fantasy

ABOUT THE AUTHOR

LJ Swallow is a USA Today bestselling paranormal romance and urban fantasy author who is the alter-ego of bestselling contemporary romance author Lisa Swallow.

Giving in to her dark side, LJ spends time creating worlds filled with supernatural creatures who don't fit the norm, and heroines who are more likely to kick ass than sit on theirs.

For more information:
ljswallow.com
lisa@lisaswallow.net

29009373R00114

Printed in Great Britain
by Amazon